**He was going to kiss her. Right here in the middle of the park.**

And she wanted him to. Desperately.

Half afraid she might be daydreaming the whole thing, and that she would snap back to attention, she curled her hand around his nape and murmured his name.

And then he was bending closer, his warm breath stirring the fine hairs on her temple.

The first touch of his lips against hers set off a chain reaction she was powerless to ignore. His elbows landed on either side of her shoulders and he lifted his head to look at her, as if trying to gauge her reaction. When he moved in again the pressure was firmer, more insistent. Nothing like the light, exploratory touch a second ago. No, his head had shifted a quarter-turn to the left, his mouth fitting perfectly over hers.

Settling in.

And she was okay with that. The fingers at his nape wandered to one of his shoulders, where the muscles bunched deliciously under her skin. All thoughts of kites and laughter were long gone. This was deadly serious—the stuff pillow talk was made of. Only Maddy didn't feel like talking. And she hoped Kaleb didn't either.

Dear Reader,

Have you ever felt responsible for a death you could have done nothing to prevent? A death that brought your whole world crashing down around you? Kaleb McBride finds himself in just such a position when he loses his only child to a terrible disease. His marriage unravels soon afterwards, and he finds himself totally alone. He shuts himself off, vowing never to have more children. And then he comes to the aid of a woman at a party who is in the middle of an asthma attack. Their attraction is immediate and explosive. Except Madeleine Grimes has a child. And a troubled past. In spite of both of those things, Kaleb soon finds himself in over his head.

Thank you for joining Kaleb and Maddy as they each struggle to let go of crushing grief and learn to enjoy life again. And maybe, just maybe, they'll discover that love is not as far out of reach as they'd thought. I hope you enjoy reading their story as much as I loved writing it!

Love,

*Tina Beckett*

# A DADDY FOR
# HER DAUGHTER

BY
TINA BECKETT

MILLS &
BOON

First published in Great Britain 2016
By Mills & Boon, an imprint of HarperCollins*Publishers*
1 London Bridge Street, London, SE1 9GF

Large Print edition 2017

© 2016 Tina Beckett

ISBN: 978-0-263-06683-8

Printed and bound in Great Britain
by CPI Antony Rowe, Chippenham, Wiltshire

Three-times Golden Heart® finalist **Tina Beckett** learned to pack her suitcases almost before she learned to read. Born to a military family, she has lived in the United States, Puerto Rico, Portugal and Brazil. In addition to travelling, Tina loves to cuddle with her pug, Alex, spend time with her family, and hit the trails on her horse. Learn more about Tina from her website, or 'friend' her on Facebook.

### Books by Tina Beckett

### Mills & Boon Medical Romance

#### *The Hollywood Hills Clinic*
*Winning Back His Doctor Bride*

#### *Midwives On-Call at Christmas*
*Playboy Doc's Mistletoe Kiss*

*The Dangers of Dating Dr Carvalho*
*To Play with Fire*
*His Girl From Nowhere*
*How to Find a Man in Five Dates*
*The Soldier She Could Never Forget*
*Her Playboy's Secret*
*Hot Doc from Her Past*

Visit the Author Profile page at millsandboon.co.uk for more titles.

To my husband,
for putting up with my weird, writerly ways!

## CHAPTER ONE

Kaleb McBride hated tuxedos.

It was safe to say that he and tuxes were no longer on speaking terms. He wore them only when it was required of him. Like tonight.

Sprinting down the steps of the Seattle Consortium Hotel, he made it a point to avoid eye contact with anyone as he dashed by. Because everywhere he looked, all he saw were costumes. Except this wasn't Halloween and the myriad assortment of outfits or lack thereof was enough to make his head swim. From Elizabethan gowns to fairy-tale characters to flappers loaded with fringe, it was the only thing like it he'd ever seen. He even skirted a lone vampire who emitted a low hiss as he strode past.

If the hospital hadn't made an agreement to

provide concierge medical care to guests at the hotel, he probably wouldn't even be here tonight.

A costume designers' masquerade party. Who on earth even thought up something like that?

A suited doorman nodded to him and motioned him through yet another velvet-lined hallway. "She's in the reception lobby."

His patient, he assumed, and the reason he'd left the hospital's swanky yearly fund-raiser—which was still trudging along without him in the hotel ballroom. Thank goodness for medical emergencies.

He burst into the lobby.

There.

Sure enough, sprawled on the floor next to a cluster of fancy potted plants was a woman dressed all in black. Shiny black.

Evidently the hospital hadn't realized they'd booked their event on the same day as this. Both were dress-up affairs, but where one was as serious as it was upscale, this one looked…well, surreal. And a whole lot more fun.

Jacques, the hotel manager, was kneeling beside the downed woman, who was lying on her stomach. What he'd decided must be a long black leotard ended in sky-high boots of the same color. Had she fallen off them? A tail was attached to a cute little tush. Something he had no business noticing.

Jacques looked up as Kaleb reached him, the relief in his eyes evident. "I think she's hyperventilating."

Even as the man said the words, a muffled sound came from his patient, a rasping roar that was much too labored for his liking.

"Let's turn her over."

A black mask that looked like a patchwork of glossy black latex bound together with white stitching covered the woman's whole head, leaving only her eyes and bright red lips exposed. Cat ears were perched on top.

The woman was dressed as a cat. A very sexy cat at that.

A quick glance could find no zipper, and the wheezing was getting steadily louder. Panicked green eyes looked up at him, one hand going to her chest as it continued to rise and fall in staccato heaves.

"We need to cut this mask off her. Now."

The roaring paused for a second before starting up again. "No." Wheeze, wheeze, wheeze. *Cough.* "…sister…kill me."

Sister? To hell with her sister. A question surged to the forefront of his mind. "Do you have asthma?"

"Yes." The rattling sound grew worse. "Albuterol. In my purse. Left at desk."

Desk?

Jacques spoke up. "Some of the guests checked their briefcases and purses in at the concierge rather than carrying them around all night." He glanced down. "Do you know your ticket number?"

The woman shook her head, gasping again. Her fingers fumbled at the wide belt encircling her waist. Kaleb spotted an opening in the side. Brushing her hands away, he felt inside and came out with a slip of paper. "Here."

Jacques grabbed it and leaped up, heading to

the desk a few feet away. In less than a minute, he came back with a black purse.

Without waiting to ask, Kaleb reached into the dark recesses of the bag and encountered a familiar-shaped object. "Got it." He pulled the canister free, giving it a couple of hard shakes to mix the contents.

*Wheeze. Cough.*

Feeling vaguely obscene, he pushed the inhaler against those red lips, his skin brushing the delicate point of her chin as her mouth wrapped around the canister.

Even as he pumped off a couple of shots of medication, it hit him how warm the lobby was. Maybe because it was packed with people. Beads of perspiration lined his own neck and face.

Between the elaborately designed costumes and the crowded conditions in the room, he was surprised he hadn't been called to treat any of the attendees before now.

Still holding the inhaler, he listened for her breathing. It immediately began to settle down, the hollow wheeze changing to a deep pull of air accompanied by a much easier exhalation.

"It's working." Her voice came out in a whisper.

She reached up and took the inhaler from him, those bright eyes glancing at his face and then skipping away just as quickly. Something sparked to life in his chest.

He couldn't know her.

Swearing to himself that he only had her best interest at heart, he cleared his throat. "We still need to get the headpiece off so you can breathe easier."

She gave a hum that he took as assent.

"Zipper?"

"Adhesive fastener. At the back." She paused, the inhaler still in her hand. "I'm sorry. I just couldn't make it to the counter to get my purse or I could have done it myself."

He could well imagine. With those heels and trying to navigate through the crowd, it would have been quite a feat under normal circumstances much less during an asthma attack.

Now that the medical crisis was easing, he was

aware that a few costumed characters had gathered around them. Probably waiting for the great unveiling.

A tiny glimmer of anticipation sizzled through his own system.

*Not the time, Kaleb.*

He helped her sit upright before reaching behind her head, finding the seam and prizing apart the edges, the sharp rip of the fastener tape as it gave way filling the air around them.

He carefully peeled the stretchy fabric forward, easing it away from her face. The second he tugged it free, he stopped dead, his inner warning system going on high alert.

His own breath sluiced from his lungs in a rush he was helpless to prevent.

It couldn't be. And yet it sure as hell looked like her. So unless she had a doppelgänger...

"Madeleine?"

From the shiny red curls—only slightly flattened by the tight mask—to the flashing warning in her eyes, there was no mistaking who she was.

One of the doctors from the hospital. His hospital.

But there was no way the Madeleine Grimes he knew would have been caught dead in an outfit like this.

Before he could even cobble together a sentence, she nodded. "It's a very long story."

"I'll bet."

"Exactly."

He blinked. "I'm sorry?"

"Nothing. My sister thought my coming here would be a good idea. She kind of dared me to... Well, she set me up on a—" her eyes went to the floor and stayed there "—blind date."

Blind date?

He just wasn't seeing it.

The glare she sent him dared him to say one word. Not likely.

How in the hell would she even be able to tell what her date looked like? Or maybe that was the point—she could be caught up in some kind of weird role-playing fetish.

Only the Madeleine Grimes he knew tended toward uptight and aloof, rather than…

Than what?

He had no idea how her sister could have talked her into climbing into that sexy costume and prowling around the lobby looking for her date. Or why Madeleine would even agree to it.

But suddenly he wanted to find out.

Wanted to understand the thought processes that had led her here. But he would only get that if…

If he got her out of here.

Before he could think better of it, he said, "And this blind date. Do you know his name?"

"Yes, it's Max Hayward." Her eyes slid away from his again. "But when I asked at the reception desk, he hadn't arrived. I think he stood me up. Not that I wasn't tempted to do the same thing."

She gave a quick lift of a shoulder. "I'm going to take everything that's happened tonight as a sign. I'll leave a note at the desk, telling him I had to leave unexpectedly, just in case."

"That's probably a good idea."

"I think so too." Taking a deep breath and blowing it out, Madeleine tilted her head back, revealing the long line of her throat. No hint of the asthma attack she'd had moments earlier. "Man, I can't wait to get out of this costume."

She reached for her elbow and peeled a long black glove down her arm, revealing pale creamy skin as she went. She did the same with the other glove. The process was…agonizing.

His muscles tightened. *Knock it off, Kaleb. It isn't like she's going to strip herself naked in front of all these people.* Although he'd had some pretty crazy thoughts when he'd slid off that mask and seen who was sitting there. The contrast between the Madeleine he thought he knew and the one in this room was a little unsettling.

Taking a hurried breath of his own, he struggled to come up with a coherent thought. "Your sister. Does she work at the hospital as well?"

"No." She gave a quick laugh, scooping her inhaler from her lap and dropping it in her purse. "She faints at the sight of blood. She's a costume designer, which is another reason I agreed to come. I was supposed to be a living advertisement for her work."

"Work. There's actually a market for…?" He gestured toward her outfit, not sure what he was asking.

"Look around you. From theater, to film, to school plays, there's always a demand for well-made and innovative costumes." She scrubbed a hand through her hair, ruffling it into an unruly mass that he found oddly appealing. Then she took one of the shiny gloves and held it up. "This is Roxy's realm, not mine."

Roxy. A fitting name for the creature in whose suit Madeleine had found herself.

And from the word *dare* she'd used earlier, Kaleb had to assume that this was not a place Roxy's sister would have chosen on her own.

"So you're here under duress?"

"Let's just say that Roxy said I needed to loosen up. She bet I wouldn't last two minutes at one of these conventions."

"And did you?"

"Yes. I would have been here an hour if something from the costume hadn't set off an attack."

He smiled and stood, offering her a hand, which she accepted, gracefully rising to her feet and adjusting the belt at her waist. "How long did you agree to stay?"

"Until the party died down. But surely she won't accuse me of cheating under the circumstances."

He tensed, hand tightening slightly on hers at the word *cheating*. Maybe because that was exactly what his ex-wife had done. He, more than anyone, understood her particular circumstances, but he'd still felt like the biggest fool on the planet when he'd discovered what she'd been doing. Hiding her grief behind a mask just as surely as Madeleine had hidden her identity behind hers.

"Do you want to run by the hospital and get checked out before finishing your night?" Releasing her hand, he braced himself to tell her goodbye. Something he should have done ten minutes ago.

"I think I'm done for the evening." This time,

it was Madeleine who smiled, and the flash of white teeth was something he wasn't used to from her. The woman was always so serious. Then again, this whole night had been like something out of one of those strange dreams. The ones where nothing made sense.

Like this surreal encounter? He glanced around again, really taking in his surroundings this time. Standing in his tuxedo in a roomful of costumed adults, Kaleb felt out of sorts. And definitely out of place. Especially when there was what looked like a deflated cat's head on the ground beside a beautiful woman.

Even as the thought went through his mind, she reached down and scooped up the mask, letting it sit in the crook of her left arm. "Thank you again. I probably would have been better off going to the hospital's fund-raiser instead. But I don't do stuffy…"

The words cut off abruptly, and her teeth sank deep into her lower lip. Rich color swept all the way to her hairline.

Kaleb allowed one side of his mouth to curve

up. "You don't 'do stuffy'—" he gestured around the room "—but you'll do this."

She laughed. And the sound cut straight to his gut. It was rich, melodic and made things tighten in awkward places. Her palms floated up and down, as if weighing her options. "Stuffed shirts or make-believe. I can't decide."

Suddenly, he wanted to hear that laugh again. He bent closer. "I would offer to take you upstairs and show you what you're missing…" When her eyes widened, he realized how the suggestion sounded. "Upstairs, as in the party going on in the fifteenth-floor ballroom."

"Oh."

Was there a tiny bit of disappointment in that single word?

Of course not. *It's all in your imagination, bud.*

"How about a cup of coffee instead? I want to make sure that asthma attack is all the way under control."

"Coffee sounds wonderful, but I can't go anywhere dressed like this. I need to go home and change." She hesitated. "I have coffee there."

He gave another half smile. "You do? Is that an invitation?"

"Well, I...I mean if you want to join me, that would be okay. And no one's there at the moment." She shook her head. "Well, I mean my cat is there, and my sister is..."

Her voice trailed away.

"Your sister is there? With the cat?"

"No."

There went those white teeth nibbling at her lower lip again. "But the coffee is there. With the cat. Right?"

"Yes. Why don't you stop by for a cup? It's the least I can do to say thank you."

"No thanks necessary, but I would love to. Especially if you won't agree to run by the hospital for a quick checkup."

Something told Kaleb he should be heading in the opposite direction, back toward the elevators...back up to the safety of the fifteenth floor, where his obligations lay. But something about seeing Madeleine in that suit made him want to find out if there were other things about her he didn't know. Not that he knew her at all. But he wanted to. If only to satisfy his curiosity. So one cup of coffee it was. And then he would be on his way back to his own life. In his own high-rise apartment.

Maddy squirmed on the beige leather seat of Dr. Kaleb McBride's luxury car. What had started out as a halfhearted invitation—one she had *not* expected him to accept—had somehow ended up with her riding beside him.

She could not believe she was bringing him—a man—to her place. It had been ages since she'd had a guy over. Well, Kaleb wasn't a guy, exactly. He was a…a colleague. She had always been tongue-tied around the resident bad boy of West Seattle Hospital, so she'd learned the hard way to keep that tongue firmly planted on the bottom of her mouth. She'd allowed one man to reduce her to a stuttering mess. Never again.

Still, she couldn't resist a quick sideways glance at the figure in the driver's seat. Then she slouched lower into the smooth upholstery.

There was a reason the nurses at West Seattle whispered about Kaleb long after he strode down their hallways.

Inky dark hair curled over the collar of the man's equally black tux, and warm brown eyes had flirted with her as easily as he flirted with every other woman at the hospital. Only Maddy had usually been immune, switching on her anti-charm force field and aiming it at any man who ventured into her personal space. So far, it had worked. Up until now. When she'd forgotten to hit that internal panic button. Thanks to her asthma. The feel of Kaleb's fingers cupping her chin as he'd administered her medication hadn't helped any.

Okay, she could explain away all of that. She'd been oxygen deprived. But what she didn't understand was why she hadn't told the man the reason Roxy wasn't at her apartment: it was because she'd gone on a girls' night out, with the person Maddy loved more than anything on this earth. Her daughter.

None of that was any of his business, right?

He was coming to her house to have a quick cup of coffee. To make sure her asthma attack really was over—just as he'd said. There was no need to tell him about Chloe. It wasn't as if her daughter were a deep dark secret. Her friends at the hospital all knew about her.

But not the circumstances surrounding her birth.

She shook off the thought. That was behind her. A year had gone by since she'd moved to this city, and she loved it here. It was huge, compared to what she was used to. She could actually get lost here. Well, not lost, but she could blend in. No one knew anything about her. Not like in the tiny town of Gamble Point, Nebraska, where you "couldn't belch without the whole county knowing about it," according to her father. She still missed him.

She needed to call her mom to let her know she was still okay. Still out of reach. She had Roxy to thank for that. Her sister had given her a precious gift: a new beginning in a brand-new city. She owed her big-time. And if putting on a slinky cat costume could help cover a little of that debt, Maddy would do it a hundred times over.

"Are you cool enough?"

"Wh—what?" She glanced over to find Kaleb fiddling with the climate-control buttons. "Oh, yes. I'm fine, thank you."

This was a stupid idea. She should just have him drop her off at the nearest corner. She could catch a cab back to her place.

But it was too late, and if she tried to explain now she'd only wind up blurting out something that would make her look like a foolish child. As if she hadn't already looked like one when he'd come across her splayed on the ground in her costume.

Debt or no debt, Roxy was going to pay for that for sure. Although watching Chloe's eyes light up when she'd seen her dressed up as a sexy cat had made the whole fiasco of an evening a little less humiliating.

"Go down two more stoplights and then turn left. My building will be on the right." In truth, she also didn't want to have to call Roxy and admit that she hadn't lasted even an hour. Barely even twenty minutes. Nor had she met her date. But none of that was her fault. Something in the costume had messed up her airways. But she had a feeling Roxy would think she'd simply wimped out on her.

Well, too bad. Maddy was a grown woman who could make her own decisions. And leaving her hometown with her daughter had been one of those decisions. Matthew hadn't even tried to follow them. Then again, he'd be arrested if he came within a hundred yards of her, according to the courts. He wasn't allowed to see Chloe. In fact, he hadn't even asked to visit her. And if Maddy had her way, he'd never get the chance. Too much tainted water had passed under that particular bridge. Her ex had never wanted to have kids in the first place…had been disgusted when *her* birth control—because he couldn't be bothered to think about those kinds of things— had failed. As her pregnant body had begun to change, his disgust had morphed into something sinister. Something…

She shook herself from her thoughts just as Kaleb pulled up to the entry of her modest apartment complex. "Is there a key code?"

"No, just push the button on the panel."

He did and the single-levered barrier went up immediately. Kaleb slid into the dark parking garage, following the reflective arrows painted on the pavement. "Could someone get into the building itself through the garage?"

She frowned. "Yes, but we haven't had any problems." At least they hadn't in the year that she'd lived there. And most of the people in the building knew each other. A stranger would be noticed.

Kind of like in her hometown? She shrugged off the thought. "There are also cameras in the garage and in the hallways." She'd been shocked by the high cost of rent and by the security measures that came with living in a big city. But she'd come to love the anonymity afforded by a city with over six hundred thousand residents.

Sliding into one of the ten guest spots, he nodded. "Glad to hear it."

Before she could twist around and reach into the backseat for the head to her sister's costume, Kaleb had already retrieved it and was out of the car, heading around to her side. Just as he opened her door, something pinged from her purse.

Ugh. Her cell phone. And she had a pretty good idea who it would be. Roxy. The last person she wanted to text with right now. She could just ignore it until she got to the safety of her apartment.

What if something was wrong with Chloe, though? She climbed from the car and freed her phone from her purse, noting Kaleb's frown as she glanced down at her screen.

"It's Roxy." She didn't know why she was explaining.

We're headed for that place with all the paraphernalia for Chloe's doll. Having a blast. Hope you are too.

A blast? Not quite. But a few of her muscles relaxed. Chloe could spend hours in that particular shop, which meant they wouldn't drop by the apartment anytime soon. She quickly typed

Okay, have fun! and then dropped the phone back into her purse. She made no mention of the fact that she was arriving home with an attractive man in tow. A man whose name was most definitely not Max, nor was he from the masquerade party.

And if she had her way, Roxy would never know that Kaleb had been here. It would be her little secret. After all, that was one thing she'd learned she was good at. Hiding the ugly truth from everyone around her.

She glanced up at Kaleb. "I'm on the fifth floor."

Modest by Seattle standards, her apartment had everything she and Chloe needed. It was only one bedroom, but she'd got around that by converting the tiny study into her daughter's bedroom. There was a park right around the corner that Chloe loved to go to, so Maddy never really felt trapped. And she couldn't afford anything bigger. Not yet. Once she'd been at the hospital a couple more years she'd be eligible for a pretty substantial raise. Maybe then they could move to a nicer place. When Chloe started elementary school, they would need something bigger. But for now, the apartment was just right.

They went into the lobby, and Maddy pressed the button on the elevator, hearing the creak as it broke free from whatever floor it was on and began to slowly descend to ground level.

"How's your breathing?"

"Fine." Even as she said it, she realized why he was asking. His proximity had caused her lungs to start working harder, wheezing a little—kind of like the elevator—as they pulled air into her lungs and then pushed it back out. To prove she was okay, she sucked in another breath and then let it rush back out. "You would never even know I'd had a problem."

Kaleb made a noise. She wasn't sure if it was a snort of doubt or if he was agreeing with her assessment. Whatever it was, she was ignoring it. Because she did not want to have to explain that having him behind her was doing a number on her organs. All of them, not just her lungs. Her swirling thoughts, jittery heartbeat and shaky legs were all warning signs.

She shouldn't have brought him here. Her apartment was her one safe place. The spot she and Chloe could be totally themselves.

The elevator arrived, spitting out a puff of chilled air as she and Kaleb stepped through the doors. Kaleb moved to the opposite wall of the compartment, and she couldn't help but smile at the sight of him carrying that cat's mask. From where she was standing, she could see quite a few strands of her hair clinging to the stark black fabric of his tux. They must have got stuck in the mask when he'd pulled it off her. "I'll have to loan you my lint roller before you leave."

When his head tilted, she nodded at his trousers. "I evidently shed as bad as a cat does."

Oh, Lord, she'd been trying to make a joke, but he probably thought she'd been eyeing his pants this whole time. "Not that I was staring. I mean…" Her words faded when she realized she was only making things worse.

His mouth cranked up on one side in a way that

made his left eye narrow slightly, craggy lines webbing out from the corner of it. Her breathing went wonky all over again before she schooled it back to normal.

Dumb, dumb, dumb. This was one of her more stupid moves.

Thankfully the elevator decided not to prolong her misery and rolled to a halt. She was across the tiny foyer as soon as the doors opened, sliding her key into the lock of her apartment.

Once inside, she took the mask from him and waved to the front room. "Make yourself at home, and I'll be right back." She zoomed into the kitchen, only to stop when Jetta went tearing past her to check out the intruder.

Oh, no! Expecting to hear curses at any moment, she headed back the way she came. But when she reached the living room, she found Kaleb on his haunches, stroking long fingers over her cat's black fur, rubbing one of his cheeks and murmuring in low tones. When she moved forward to pick the animal up, Kaleb again beat her to it, scooping up the young feline and tucking him into the crook of his arm. "I take it this is the cat in question?"

Her cat was not a fan of being sandwiched in someone's arms, but right now he looked as if he was anything but unhappy. "Yes. His name is Jetta."

"Jetta. It fits him." He moved to a corner of the sofa and lowered himself into it, still stroking the cat. More shedding hair for his tux, but the man didn't seem to mind a bit. Nor did Jetta, who was lapping up the attention. "Do you want any help? With the coffee?"

She was staring again.

"Oh. Um, no. I've got it." She started back for the kitchen before turning toward her visitor. "How do you like it?"

"Hot and sweet." That crazy tilted smile went off again. "My coffee, that is."

Yikes. A shiver went through her.

"I understood what you meant."

How lame could she get? Evidently very, judging from her answers so far. She picked up the pace, practically skidding around the corner into the kitchen, where she leaned against the wall and drew several deep breaths, hand over her heart.

For twenty seconds she remained that way, eyes closed, wondering what it would be like for Kaleb to undress with those strands of her hair still attached to his clothing. Oh, Lord, she'd better get that image out of her head pronto. And she was still in her cat suit. Maybe she had time to run back to her bedroom and change. While she was there, she could call out to him in a seductive voice and ask him to—

"Madeleine? Are you okay?" Fingers touched her hair and her eyelids jerked apart.

Horrified that he'd found her daydreaming about him, she rattled around for a response before she noticed he had her purse in his hands. She'd left it in the entryway.

"I'm fine. Is something wrong?" Funny she should ask that question, because something was wrong. With this whole scene. She hadn't been affected by a man in years, and this wasn't the time to start.

"Your phone pinged. I thought it might be something important."

Taking the purse from him with shaking fingers, she reached in and took her phone.

Chloe wants to run home to get her doll so she can try on the clothes. We'll swing by and grab it and then head on our way. Hope you're having fun at the party!

Her sister was coming here. Now. Oh, no! She was bound to get the wrong idea! And worse, Maddy didn't want Chloe seeing her in their home with a strange man.

Kaleb must have seen something in her face, because he took a step closer. "What is it?"

"My sister is coming over. She'll be here in about ten minutes."

His brows went up. "And you'd rather she not find me here."

"I know it sounds weird and crazy—"

"This whole evening has been an interesting mixture of weird and crazy. But I understand, and I'll see myself out. Just one question." Tilted smile came back for another visit. "What exactly does a person wear under a cat costume?"

Maddy laughed. Partly at the audacity of the question and partly at the irony of her answer. Not that he would see her in her black leotard. In another life, this might have ended differently. Parts of her were warming up, and she'd love nothing better than to explore a quick no-strings dalliance with a man who was too handsome for his own good. And for hers.

"They wear a catsuit. What else?"

"What else, indeed." He twirled a strand of her hair one last time, before leaning in and kissing her cheek. "I'll see myself out, Madeleine Grimes. But I would like a rain check for that coffee."

"Okay." She waited for what seemed like forever before she heard her front door click softly shut. And then she sank to the floor a shaking mass of fear, relief…and disappointment.

# CHAPTER TWO

WHAT WAS HE doing here?

He wasn't sure. Respiratory Therapy was two floors above where his office was located. Part of his job was in the hospital itself, but he had to be ready to leave for the luxury hotel across the street at a second's notice. Or one of its sister hotels, which were sprinkled around the city.

The hospital had partnered with the swanky investment group, and, honestly, it suited him perfectly. He'd never liked being trapped in the sterile confines of a hospital. Too many bad memories. When his life had taken a turn for the worse, Kaleb had had to endure the pitying glances of colleagues and nursing staff until the bitter end, when his wife—also a nurse—had had an affair with another doctor. It had been the final tragic straw in a marriage that had been spiraling downhill.

So why was he walking across the floor to see a woman who had caught his attention in the strangest of ways? Maybe because he didn't quite believe the surreal experience had actually happened. And because the image of the woman lounging around in something akin to a slinky black wet suit had haunted his dreams for the past two nights. And then her mention of a catsuit. He'd had to look up what that was. And while he was pretty sure some of the images hadn't been what Madeleine meant by the term, he would have loved to have been there when she stripped herself down to it.

He was here to assure himself that the Madeleine he was acquainted with was indeed the cool, aloof woman he'd known before that asthma attack. And to make sure she really was okay. She'd acted shaken the whole time he'd been in her apartment, and if her sister hadn't been on her way home, he might have insisted she get checked out.

Arriving in front of the door of her office, he hesitated, wondering if he should turn around and head back to the safety of his own corner of the hospital. But he was here now. And if he left now, the nurse he'd asked about her whereabouts was bound to ask Madeleine if he'd found her.

And then she—and the other nurse—would wonder why he'd left without seeing her. Better to just go through with it.

He knocked.

"Yes? Come in." The soft voice from two nights ago was now infused with a crispness that Kaleb definitely recognized from other chance meetings, where she'd given him a clipped "hello" that had been anything but friendly.

Even then, though, their interactions had intrigued him. She'd been indifferent to his presence, no sign of the half invitations he'd got from a few of the other single women in the hospital. Curiosity had had him trying to break through that reserve whenever he saw her. But he'd never glimpsed the slightest chink in her armor.

Until her asthma attack.

He opened the door and stepped through it. She wasn't with a patient. Instead she sat at a desk with two simple chairs in front of it. The work surface was surprisingly devoid of any clutter, as was the room itself, giving off an almost austere vibe. Her fingers rested on the keyboard of a laptop, and a framed picture, its back turned to him, sat on the right-hand corner.

If he were smart, he'd toss a quick question about her health and leave. But he didn't. And the slight widening of her eyes as she looked up told him that he was the last person she'd expected to see that morning.

They were even, then. Because she'd been the last person he'd expected to see beneath that cat costume at the convention.

"Did your sister make it to your place okay the other night?"

Her eyes shifted from his before coming back again. "Oh…um, yes, thank you. I appreciated your help at the hotel."

"Just doing my job."

And had he just been doing his job when he'd

driven her home and installed himself on her couch with her cat? Hell, no. He'd wanted to be there.

He'd wanted to stay, actually. Which was crazy.

"Of course you were. But I'm still glad you happened to be there."

Damn. He'd sounded like an ass without meaning to. "I came by to make sure you're okay. No lasting problems from the asthma attack?"

"None." She smiled, and a slight warmth infused it. "I'm a pulmonologist. I've given myself the all clear to return to work."

He smiled back. "Is that why you went into pulmonary medicine? Your asthma?"

"No." She hesitated. "That was because of my younger sister. She had cystic fibrosis. She died two years ago."

His insides tightened at the sadness in her eyes.

Kaleb wasn't the only one who'd known loss— who'd had someone special succumb to disease. No one ever expected it to happen to them, though. "I'm sorry."

"It's okay. We miss her terribly, but we were

so lucky to have had her with us as long as we did. Patricia was sweet and funny, and we loved her very much." Her hands clasped on her desk. "Roxy and I were both tested to see if we're carriers of the disease. Thank God we're not."

Carriers. Pain wrenched through his gut.

At least she and Roxy had lucked out.

Maddy reached for the picture and angled it a little more toward her. A photo of her dead sister?

Trying to erase the whole subject of genetic testing from his head, he threw out the first question that came to mind. "Are your parents still living?"

She motioned to one of the chairs. "My mom is. My dad died in a tractor accident on their farm in Nebraska a few years ago."

"I'm sorry again. Is your mom still working the farm?"

"She has people who do that for her." She turned around and retrieved a carafe on the credenza behind her desk. "I can finally offer you that cup of coffee, if you still want one?"

If she was offering, she must not be in too much

of a hurry to get rid of him. He rounded one of the chairs and settled into it, not quite sure why he was in such a hurry to stay. "Only if you're having a cup as well."

"I am." Standing, she poured coffee into two plain white mugs and handed him one. "It should still be hot. As for the sweet…" She pushed a sugar bowl across the desk.

So she remembered his words. He hadn't been himself that night. Then again, he hadn't been in a beautiful woman's home in quite a while either. His encounters tended to happen at hotels or at his place. The leaving was too awkward otherwise. His instinct was to make his exit as soon as the act was over. And that didn't pose as much of a problem when it was at his apartment. Maybe because it was his territory and there was no need to try to choose a time frame. He left that up to the woman. As long as she left. So far, it hadn't been an issue. The women he chose to spend time with were just as anxious to keep things simple and fluid. It was easier that way for both of them.

He spooned a teaspoon of sugar into his cup

and stirred it, ignoring the familiar pang that occurred whenever he thought too much about the past. About his part in the failure of his marriage.

"What about you?" she asked. "Any siblings?"

"Nope. I'm an only child." He smiled. "And my parents are both alive and live here in Seattle." No need to tell her about Grace. Or Janice. Or the divorce. Theirs had been a fairy-tale wedding—without the fairy-tale ending.

Madeleine touched the picture frame again. Maybe it was just a nervous habit. Or a way to ease the discomfort of having him in her office.

But why would it make her uncomfortable?

She hadn't completely gone back to the stiff demeanor she'd adopted every time he'd seen her in the past. She still seemed incredibly warm, including the deep red curls, which were now very much loose and free around her head and neck. He remembered twining one around his finger two nights ago in her kitchen, just as his eyes had dropped to her lips. Thank goodness she'd read her text or he would have kissed her right then and there. To hell with knowing who she was. She'd been affected as well. He'd seen it in the dilation of her pupils as he'd stepped closer. If not for her sister, the night might have ended very differently.

Thank goodness for small miracles. He took a bracing sip of his coffee, watching her. "Are you going to the staff meeting?"

She glanced at her watch and then blinked. "I didn't realize it was almost that time. Yes, I'm going. They're discussing budgets and I want to make sure my department is covered." She took a drink of her own brew. He noticed she took it black. The coffee was dark and strong, just how he liked it.

"Mind if I go down with you? My budget doesn't work quite the same way as the other departments, but I still like to make sure I know what's going on."

"That's right. You do concierge medicine."

Surely she already knew that. Because he sure as hell had already known what department she worked in the second that cat head had come off.

Why would he think she knew anything about him? Was it a hit to his ego that someone might not know who he was? Maybe he should find out.

"Did you know it was me in that hotel lobby, Madeleine?" He took another deep pull on his coffee.

"It's Maddy." Her glance flitted away, her cheeks turning pink. "And, yes, of course I recognized you."

Maddy. It fit her. Then again, so did her full name. It was as if she had more than one personality wrapped up in that cute little body. He sat back and crossed his foot over his knee. He also liked that she wanted him to use the shortened version of her name, although he had no idea why.

And why had she blushed? Maybe she hadn't liked being caught in a vulnerable moment, like during her asthma attack. Who could blame her? He wouldn't have cared for being in that position either. "Does Roxy have asthma as well?"

"No. She's as strong as an ox. Healthwise, anyway." Madeleine said it with a twist to her mouth that made him wonder. Did she consider herself lacking in that area?

There were still things about her that intrigued him.

Just then there was some kind of commotion in the hallway. A patient emergency?

He set his coffee down and started to get up when something hit the door to Maddy's office, causing it to shudder.

"Hey, wait! You can't go in there."

Kaleb was on his feet in an instant, heading to the door. Someone—a man—stood right outside, looking behind him at whoever had yelled. Kaleb flipped the lock, just as the doorknob twisted from the outside. His senses went on high alert.

"I said stop!"

"What is it?" Maddy stood, gripping the wooden surface of her desk with both hands.

"Call Security. Now."

Her face turned white, but she picked up her cell phone and pressed the keys.

Kaleb turned back to the door, just as the man planted a hand on either side of the small rectangular window. Something glinted in one of those hands.

Things moved in slow motion. Maddy's voice asking someone to send help. The man staring into the office. Crazed eyes zeroing in on Kaleb and then something behind him. Kaleb's head swiveled to look and found Maddy. The phone fell from her fingers onto the desk, her face filled with fear.

And recognition.

"Oh, my God! Matthew!"

Maddy couldn't believe what she was seeing, even as her ex-husband's mouth tightened into a straight line.

"Open this goddamn door, Madeleine!" The rage in his voice made her take a quick step back. Her calf caught the chair behind her and she stumbled, falling into the seat.

Matthew raised his hand, pointing something— *oh, God, a gun!*—and then she was hit with a force that felt like a truck, knocking her sideways out of the chair. Every bit of breath left her body as she slammed to the ground. The glass in Chloe's picture frame shattered into a thousand pieces as it landed beside her.

Pressure against her chest made it hard to breathe and impossible to move. It took her a second to realize it wasn't from taking a hit from a bullet, but from the man who was on top of her, his body over hers as he kept her pinned down behind her desk.

Matthew was here. In the hospital. And he had a gun.

*Chloe!* Where was Chloe?

She struggled against Kaleb's weight, needing to get up.

Her phone! It was about ten feet away from the desk. She scrabbled for it, trying to turn sideways so she could drag herself toward it.

"Kaleb, oh, God, please, get off me!" The need to get to her daughter and make sure her ex-husband hadn't somehow found her gave her almost superhuman strength.

"Wait. Just wait." He pinned her wrists and held

her down, even as she wrenched against him with all her strength.

A loud bang sounded and the glass in her office door sprayed everywhere, stinging her cheek, the noise a thousand times louder than the glass in the picture frame had been.

The muted shouts she'd heard earlier amplified, becoming horrifyingly real.

Matthew was trying to get into her office. Screaming obscenities, demanding she open the door.

A second or two later, a sharp report reverberated the air around her, the echo seeming to go on forever.

Kaleb stiffened.

Had he been hit?

Then it stopped. All of it. Matthew's voice was silent, although she heard screaming and crying in the distance. She lay there, still struggling to breathe, a familiar band tightening across her lungs. She tried to say something to Kaleb, to ask him if he was okay, but the words came out as a strangled cough.

She tried again. Another hoarse cough.

*Not now. Oh, please, not now.*

Kaleb lifted off her—very much alive—but she was too involved in her current struggle to breathe to let him know how glad she was.

"Stay here."

No. She had to get to Chloe. As Kaleb went to the door, she crawled toward her phone, sucking down what little air she could as she went.

She turned the phone over. Broken. The cracked screen was dark and empty. Panicked tears formed, and she tried to get up, but she still couldn't catch her breath.

Then Kaleb was back beside her. "Where's your inhaler?"

She pointed at the bottom drawer of her desk. She couldn't do this. Not now, when Matthew could be anywhere. She had to get to Chloe.

"Don't move." Keeping his eyes on her, Kaleb found her canister and handed it to her. She pumped the medicine into her mouth, pulling it into her aching lungs.

It took a few seconds for the bronchodilator to work its magic.

"Where...where is he? Is—is he gone?"

Oh, God, even now he could be heading to her daughter's preschool. That gun—

Another knock at the door had Maddy tensing all over again.

"Dr. McBride? Are you and Dr. Grimes okay?"

Kaleb unlocked the door, letting the hospital security guard in. "We're fine." He glanced outside. "Oh, hell."

Maddy forced her feet underneath her, but Kaleb held up a hand.

"Don't come over here. Not yet."

The guard glanced her way. "We have the hospital on lockdown, and the police are en route. Do you know the man who did this?"

"Yes. Is he still here?" Something about the look on his face...

An eerie premonition set in. She didn't want to look. Didn't want to go over there, but of course she had to. Had to see what had happened.

In the background, Maddy heard sirens. Glass

crunched under her feet as she made her way toward the door. The window still held jagged fragments of glass, and blood stained the bottom section. There was more blood along the door as if Matthew had reached through and tried to find the lock.

Maddy shuddered.

With a swallow, she started for the hallway, feeling Kaleb's hand on her shoulder as she came even with him. He gave a slight squeeze, stopping her from going any farther. It was then that she saw why.

Matthew lay sprawled on the ground, eyes staring upward at the ceiling. Only he wasn't staring. The gaze was unfocused. Unknowing. A gun was clutched in his hand. A few medical staff were gathered around him, but they weren't trying to resuscitate him or administer aid.

Because he was dead.

Bile rose to her throat. Even though it was useless, Maddy fell to her knees beside him. Forced herself to reach for his neck to see if there was a pulse, but there was too much blood and her fingers slipped off. The hole in his left temple told her all she needed to know.

Kaleb helped her to her feet. "He's gone."

The security guard repeated his question. "Do you know him?"

"He...he's my husband."

Kaleb visibly stiffened, and she realized what she'd said. "My ex-husband. He...he..." She stopped and tried to collect her thoughts. "He was in Nebraska. He wasn't supposed to find out where I was."

She glanced up at the guard. "Did anyone else get hurt?"

"No." The older man looked as pale as she felt. "He shot himself just as I drew my weapon. I would have shot him. I had no choice."

She took a step toward him, shock still muddying her thoughts. "It's okay. I'm glad he didn't hurt anyone else."

Kaleb handed her a paper towel, and she wiped the blood from her hands. Her cheek still stung, but not as much as her heart.

Chloe's father was dead. She still couldn't believe what he'd done. He'd hurt her in the past, but he'd never pulled a knife or a gun. He'd always claimed to hate her—to be glad she and Chloe were out of his life. And yet here he was. Dead. A gun on the floor beside him.

The police appeared seconds later, saying something to the security guard. One of the officers shot her a look and came over. "This man is your ex-husband? Any chance he had someone else with him?"

Maddy shook her head. "I don't think so. But I don't know for sure."

The man gave orders to the rest of the officers and they headed off in different directions. Two of the nurses standing to the side were holding each other, eyes red. One of them had a phone to her ear.

A phone!

"I have to call someone." The words came out of her throat in a shrill rush.

"Who?" The officer, a big burly guy, narrowed his eyes at her.

Possibilities rolled through her head. She could

call the school. No, she didn't want to scare Chloe. Roxy. She should call her sister. Maddy was pretty sure the police were not going to let her or anyone else out of the hospital until they fully understood what had happened.

"My sister."

He gave a curt nod. "I'll be back to ask you some questions in a few minutes."

Kaleb handed her his phone. Her fingers shook as she tried to remember her sister's phone number. Everything was programmed into her cell phone, so she didn't have to dial it under normal circumstances. She finally pulled a string of digits together, and hoping they were the right ones, she pressed the call button.

Pictures were being taken of her ex-husband's body, although it seemed horrible for him to be immortalized that way. The sourness in her throat rose even higher.

Three rings and her sister answered. "Hello?"

"Roxy, it's Maddy."

"Hey, hon, what's up?"

"Matthew was here."

"What? Where?"

"At the hospital. He had a gun." A wobble in her voice made her pause. "He's dead. He killed himself."

"Oh, God. Chloe?"

"I don't know. They won't let me leave."

"I'm on my way to the school. I'm sure she's fine. He wouldn't know where to find her."

Maddy closed her eyes, whispering, "I didn't think he could find *me* either."

"She's okay. Someone would have called by now, otherwise. I'll let you know as soon as I get there and see her with my own two eyes."

"Thank you."

She ended the call and glanced up to find Kaleb leaning against the wall, watching her. Was there suspicion in his eyes?

That was crazy. This was all Matthew's doing.

Sarah, one of the nurses, came over and touched her arm. "Are you okay, Maddy?"

Okay? No, she was far from okay, although she nodded, wrapping her arms around her middle. "I'm so sorry for all of this."

"It's not your fault."

Wasn't it? Knowing this man had put all of their lives in danger.

Matthew. Who was now dead. Why? *Why?* He'd left her alone for over a year. Not a phone call. Not a letter in all that time. And suddenly he was here. With a gun. To what? Kill her? Kill Chloe?

Renewed panic filled her system. "I have to go."

"We're on lockdown, Maddy," Kaleb reminded her. "They're not letting anyone in or out of the hospital."

Someone arrived with a long black bag, and two men lifted her ex-husband and laid him inside, zipping it closed.

A sob rose in her throat.

Taking hold of her arm, Kaleb eased her away from Sarah and everyone else, guiding her back into her office. His big body seemed to fill the space. She took a quick step back.

Kaleb frowned. "It's okay."

*Okay?* Why did everyone keep using that word?

Right now she wasn't sure anything would be okay ever again. She'd thought she'd got over her fear. Thought maybe she could finally have a normal life. Had even thought that she and Kaleb might be able to…

No. She did not need to get involved with a man.

Especially not after what had just happened. Right now all she needed was to know that her daughter was safe.

"I have to go." She repeated the words, knowing she probably sounded foolish. But she couldn't help it.

"You told the officer your ex was acting alone. Are you sure of that? Could he be part of some organization?"

Organization? It took her a minute to realize what that meant.

"He's not a terrorist. He's just a boy from a hick town who…" Her voice caught. When she tried to force out the rest of the sentence, it caught again.

Then Kaleb's arms came around her, pressing her head into his shoulder as a second sob hit her throat. Then a third. And a fourth. She couldn't believe any of this was happening. A man she'd once loved was dead. A man she'd slept with. Laughed with. Had a baby with.

A man who'd turned cruel beyond belief as time had gone on.

She had to call her mom and tell her before she heard it from somewhere else.

But first she had to get ahold of herself. She curled her hands into the soft fabric of Kaleb's shirt, the comforting scent of his body washing over her. His fingers cupped the back of her head, moving in small soothing brushes that did what her mind couldn't seem to do: returned her to the here and now. Edging back slightly, she tilted her head to look up at him. "I was so scared."

He pressed his forehead to hers. "It's okay. You're allowed to be."

Wet spots on the crisp blue of his shirt, along with twin black smudges from her mascara, made her eyes prickle all over again. She brushed at the moisture with one hand. "Your shirt. I'll pay to have it cleaned."

"It's nothing. It'll wash right out."

Random thoughts spiraled through her head.

How did he know it would wash out? Had he held crying women often?

Or had he *made* them cry? Like her ex.

No. She might not know Kaleb very well, but he was nothing like Matthew. She would have heard something from Sarah or the other nurses. Hospital grapevines let nothing go by unnoticed.

Why hadn't she heard back from Roxy yet? It had been fifteen minutes at least.

Matthew had hated Chloe. He'd had a jealous streak, even before they'd got married. Back then it had seemed innocent enough. But it had only got worse with time. Until it had no longer been amusing or flattering...but dangerous. And it had finally extended to the child she'd carried. That had been the last straw. She'd divorced him, but trying to live in the same town with his threats and middle-of-the-night phone calls had finally got to be too much. She'd filed for—and been granted—a restraining order. And then when Chloe had turned three, Maddy had decided to leave Gamble Point and move, giving in to Roxy's pleas to get away from him once and for all.

Only it didn't look as if that had worked.

She realized she was still standing far too close to Kaleb. She stepped to the side. "I had no idea he was capable…I'm sorry you got caught in the middle of this."

What if Matthew had started shooting up the place? Kaleb, as well as others, could have been injured. Or killed. She shuddered again.

Instead, Matthew had taken his own life.

He shook his head. "I'm glad I was here." His throat moved for a second. "It could have been much worse."

Exactly what she'd been thinking.

His phone chirped, and her heart leaped to her throat as she watched him press the button.

"Yes, she's right here." He handed her the phone. "It's your sister."

"Roxy?"

"It's okay. Chloe's with me. She's safe. He didn't come here."

"Thank God. Have you talked to Mom?" She

closed her eyes, fingers tight on the phone. "I was so afraid he might…"

"I called her as soon as I got Chloe. She's in shock. But she's not hurt. We're headed to your place now."

"I'll be there as soon as I can."

There was a pause, and then her sister's voice came back through. "How about you? Are you okay?"

Maddy glanced at Kaleb. "I'm shaken up, but I'm not hurt."

"I still can't believe it."

"Me either." In fact, it was hard to wrap her mind around what she'd seen today.

"Don't worry about Chloe. I won't let her out of my sight. See you when you get to the house, okay? Love you."

"Love you too."

She handed the phone back to Kaleb just as the police motioned for them to join them. It seemed as if questions were thrown at her for hours, but it couldn't have been that long. At some point, Kaleb swabbed the cut on her cheek and pressed an adhesive bandage over it. Eventually, the lock-down was called off, glass was swept up, the floor was mopped clean, and patients were allowed back into the unit.

Through it all, a steady stream of staff members came over to hug her or offer kind words, including the hospital administrator, who was making the rounds and letting everyone know that a counselor would be made available to anyone who felt they needed it.

The same officer who'd let her make her phone call came over to say goodbye. "We'll call you if we have more questions. And we'll need you to come down in the next day or two and sign a statement."

"I understand."

The man paused, then looked her in the eye. "I'm sorry for your loss."

The words were meant to be kind, but with them came a sense of relief. Because although she was sorry that Matthew had killed himself, she wasn't sorry that the threat of what he might do was gone. He would never be able to reach out and hurt his daughter. She was glad that he'd aimed his fury at her and no one else.

Still, she thanked the officer and asked him to call her when they were ready for her to sign that statement. Then he strode toward the elevator.

Tomorrow there would still be talk, and maybe for a few weeks after that, but the horror of today would hopefully fade. Maybe once the glass in her office door was replaced.

But would her guilt? None of this would have happened if she had followed her head rather than her heart all those years ago. Her hands clenched at her sides.

"Don't." Kaleb's voice came to her, reminding her he was still there. Still beside her.

She looked at him. "Don't what?"

"Blame yourself for this. I can see the wheels turning." He touched one of her hands.

She sucked down a deep breath, forcing her fingers to relax. "He was my ex-husband."

"Did you tell him to come here and do what he did?"

"No, but—"

"No buts. This was all on him." He gave her arm a gentle squeeze. "Seriously, are you okay?"

She shook her head. "No. But I will be. I have to be."

"Do you want me to drive you home?"

"No. I have my car."

His glance brushed over her face. "You're sure?"

"I am. Thank you again." She hesitated. "If you hadn't locked that door when you had…"

She could be dead. Matthew hadn't come to the hospital just to talk to her. Not with a gun. If Kaleb hadn't secured the door, he could have charged right into the room and shot her. And then what would have happened to Chloe?

"It worked out." He followed her into her office and glanced at the items that had fallen onto the floor when he'd sailed across her desk to get to her. "I'm sorry about your phone and laptop." The screen had detached from the keyboard and was lying next to the wall. He picked up the pieces and put them on the desk, along with her ruined cell phone.

"It's nothing." And really it wasn't, compared to everything that could have happened.

Then she picked up the framed picture of Chloe. Just a little while ago she'd been trying to hide it from Kaleb for reasons that weren't entirely clear to her. Even when she was on the phone with Roxy, she hadn't mentioned Chloe's name. Why? Was she trying to protect her daughter? Or herself in the face of a handsome man?

Kaleb nodded at the frame, a frown between his brows. "Your sister?"

Sister? Oh, Patricia.

It would be so easy to say yes, that it was a picture of her late sister as a child. But she wouldn't. Because none of it mattered anymore.

"No. It's not my sister. It's Chloe." There was a long pause. "My daughter."

# CHAPTER THREE

MADDY HAD A DAUGHTER?

Four days later, on his way to see a patient, Kaleb was still dumbfounded. He'd wondered what kinds of other things she had hidden beneath that cool exterior. Well, now he knew. She had a child.

It should make it even easier to keep his distance, but it didn't. It made it harder. Especially when the news media kept replaying the story over and over. The hospital had hired additional security guards and were installing more cameras at the entrances.

He had an ex who had done some pretty terrible things, but he certainly couldn't picture Janice coming to the hospital in hopes of killing him.

And Maddy had been terrified for her child. He remembered her trying to get to her phone when he'd pinned her under the desk. How she'd been desperate to make a call. She'd been frantic that she might have lost her daughter that day.

Kaleb knew the exact moment he'd lost his daughter. It hadn't been to a crazed gunman, but it had been to a killer nonetheless. No, he'd lost his sweet little girl to an aggressive cancer, the disease yanking the life from her body almost before he'd got to know her.

Only Kaleb had no pictures of her scattered around his apartment. They were all hidden deep in a closet. He couldn't bear to look at them. And maybe that was the reason Janice hadn't been able to look at him. But she'd sure been able to look at someone else.

*Forget about it.* Dwelling on things he couldn't change did no one any good.

He strode into the hotel and stopped at the desk. "Which room?"

"One thirty. Marian Jennings. She thinks she's having a reaction to some pain meds she received after surgery."

One of the things that places like the Seattle Consortium were good at was keeping their guests' private lives private. That included helping sequester them after surgeries and procedures. Patients were now going to fancy hotels that had spa-like atmospheres to recover. With room service and someone at their beck and call twenty-four hours a day, it was the perfect setup. Especially with concierge medicine to help ease the way.

Kaleb went up in the elevator, doing his best to forget what had happened at the hospital, but it wasn't easy. Maddy's face kept coming to mind, the terror he'd seen in it. Then there was the crazed look of her ex-husband as he'd stared at them through that window. The man had wanted to kill her. It had been there in his eyes. If Kaleb hadn't been there, would Maddy still be alive?

Something else he needed to stop dwelling on. Kaleb found the room and knocked on the door.

"Yes?"

"Dr. McBride here to see Marian Jennings."

A man opened the door. Tall and thin with a nervous twitch beneath one eye, he ushered

Kaleb into the room. "It's my wife. She's breaking out in hives. We think it might be from one of her medications."

Propped up in a huge bed, the petite woman had a bandage wrapped over her head and under her chin. Both of her eyes were black and swollen.

Plastic surgery. He'd seen it many times here. Some of them were done at West Seattle and some at other hospitals, but it didn't matter. He moved toward her, shifting his bag from one hand to the other in order to shake hers. "I'm Kaleb McBride, Ms. Jennings. Nice to meet you."

The woman nodded. "I'm sorry to call you but…" She held out one of her arms, and, sure enough, a rash had spread across the surface. "My husband was worried."

"Is this everywhere?"

"Yes, it's also on my stomach and my legs."

Kaleb frowned. "Any trouble swallowing?"

"No. None."

He took down the name of her surgeon and checked the medication the woman was on. The amoxicillin caught his attention. A common antibiotic, it could sometimes cause a rash. "Have you ever had an allergic reaction to any kind of penicillin?"

"Not that I know of."

Taking her arm, he examined the spots. "Any itchiness at all? Tingling anywhere?"

"No."

He nodded. "I don't think it's anything serious. Sometimes antibiotics, especially amoxicillin, can cause a harmless rash."

Her husband came over and placed a hand on his wife's shoulder. "So it's nothing to worry about?"

"Not at this point. We normally see itching or tingling in a true allergic reaction. I'll contact Dr. Porter's office just in case and let him know what's going on. I'll have him call you if he wants to make a change in your medication. If you see anything else, though, please don't hesitate to call me or the hospital."

The hotel's location made it convenient to do just that. It was another of the reasons they'd chosen to have the fund-raiser at the hotel. Where he'd come across Maddy in the middle of her asthma attack.

Who would have guessed that days later she'd be the target of a crazed ex-husband?

*Shake it off, Kaleb.*

He made the call to Dr. Porter's office while he was in the room with his patient and marked down his own findings on his tablet, including the room number for billing purposes. Then he excused himself after handing them his business card and reminding them to call him if they had any other problems.

He checked with the front desk to make sure there were no other calls right now and headed back across the street to the hospital. A police car out front made his muscles tense for a second, but the officer inside the vehicle didn't seem worried. It was another of the precautions the city had taken—upping the police presence in the area.

As he made his way inside, a little girl with a doll clutched under her arm rushed past him, followed by a slender woman with long blond hair. "Chloe, slow down. You need to wait for me."

Chloe?

He looked a little harder, and, sure enough, the girl had red hair and pink cheeks as she turned and grinned at the woman following her. High heels made it hard for the blonde to keep up with the child, but it didn't look as if the girl was being deliberately naughty. She was just on a mission.

"Please hurry, Aunt Roxy. I want to show her to Mommy."

Kaleb lengthened his stride, pulling alongside the pair. "I'm sorry, but are you looking for Dr. Grimes? Madeleine Grimes?"

The woman caught up with the little girl and pulled her to a halt, using an arm around her shoulders to keep her close. She then turned and looked at Kaleb. Maybe *looked* wasn't the right word. Glared was more like it. "And who are you?"

She was worried. Not angry. And Kaleb could certainly understand why after what had happened. "I work here. I'm Kaleb McBride."

She looked closer. "You're the man who helped Maddy, during…" She glanced down at her charge and then took two steps forward until she and Chloe were directly in front of him. "She told me what you did. I owe you. Big-time. It's like you were meant to be there."

"Well, I don't know about that."

"Oh. I do." She looked at him with new eyes. "Would you mind taking me to Maddy's office? This hospital is so huge, I always end up getting lost, and we're supposed to have lunch together." She gave him a meaningful look. "She's been worried. Ever since. And she feels guilty, even though she tries to hide it."

Kaleb didn't like the idea of Maddy living in fear and guilt. But he knew from experience that trauma could last long after the event was over. Maybe she should talk to the counselor the hospital had hired.

"I'll be happy to."

The little girl, who'd been silent up to this point, evidently decided he wasn't a threat. "Hi.

I'm Chloe." She held up a naked doll that was half her size. "And this is Patsy."

Roxy rolled her eyes. "I tried to talk her into putting clothes on her, but—"

"Mommy has to choose her lunch outfit."

The woman lifted a large shopping bag emblazoned with the name of a doll company and gave an amused smile. "Yes, and we have Patsy's entire wardrobe with us, right down to six pairs of shoes. And a cat costume."

Kaleb smiled. "Maddy told me you were a costume designer."

"She did, did she?" Roxy glanced at him again, brows up.

"I saw her at the convention."

Those arched brows went even higher. "*You* were at the masquerade party?"

"Not exactly." Evidently Maddy hadn't told her sister what had happened with the costume. "I was there for the hospital fund-raiser on the fifteenth floor."

"So how did you see her at the convention?

She wasn't out of costume, was she? That's a big no-no."

"We…left together."

There. That was the best he could do without spilling the beans.

"Oooooh!" Roxy expanded that single syllable until he thought she was going to pass out from lack of oxygen.

Chloe tipped her doll, cradling it in her arms like a baby. "I can't wait to see Mommy. Is her office far?"

Kaleb's attention came back to the little girl with a bump as he tried not to think about how much he missed these kinds of conversations, back when life was normal and good. He'd better just take the pair to Maddy's office, so he could be on his way. "No, not too far. If you'll follow me, I'll show you where she is."

The whole way up the elevator, Chloe kept up a running commentary on what she wanted to have for lunch. Probably three or four years old, with huge shining eyes and a quick smile, she was certainly a charmer. And a talker. His own

Grace had been quiet and reserved. But she'd been the love of his life.

He clenched his jaw and tried not to do what he did every day. Attempt to draw up the memory of his daughter's face only to have his brain glitch and fumble the pieces until they were impossible to fit together. Which was probably why he should have a few snapshots on his mantel at home. But it just hurt too much to see her healthy and alive, when at the end she'd been so very ill.

It was also hard to listen to another little girl having the conversations that Grace should have been able to have. If she'd lived past the age of two.

They arrived on Maddy's floor, and he started down the hallway, only to feel a small hand grab his. The tension in his body ramped up to an all-time high. He glanced over at Maddy's sister to find Roxy fixing him with a speculative gleam that was even more pointed. And ridiculous. He and Maddy were not hooking up.

Although he had to admit the thought had crossed his mind more than once the first time he'd seen her emerge from the head of that costume. But she'd just lived through a horrifying experience. The last thing she wanted or needed was a superficial one-night stand.

And she had a young daughter. Another big strike against the idea. Not just because it wasn't easy to find alone time with a child in tow, but because Kaleb's insides were twisted in knots from just this short encounter with Chloe.

If he were smart, he would just point the pair in the direction of Maddy's office and send them on their way, but that would mean he would have to shake off the little girl's grip, and he didn't want to do that. But once she let go of him to hug her mother, he could simply withdraw and leave them to it.

Before he could knock on the door, though, it opened, and a woman stepped into the hallway, followed by Maddy. She stopped whatever she'd been saying midsentence to look at him.

"Hi, Mommy!"

Chloe's excited greeting caused her glance to slide down Kaleb's arm until it collided with her daughter. Then her eyes jumped back to his before returning to her patient. Confusion changed to a darker emotion.

She placed a protective hand on the little girl's head, her voice calm and collected as she finished giving her instructions to the woman, but there'd been a moment of horror in her gaze when she'd realized he was holding Chloe's hand. Because of what had happened with Matthew almost a week ago?

Kaleb opened his hand to try to release the girl's, but the little girl's fingers stubbornly squeezed tighter. Roxy was practically crowing with delight on the other side of him, despite her sister's obvious discomfort. He ignored her.

After walking a few more steps with her patient, Maddy reminded the woman to call if she had any questions or concerns. And then all her attention swiveled back to them. She squatted on her haunches and held out her arms. Right on cue, Chloe thrust the still-naked doll into Kaleb's hands and leaped into her mother's embrace. "You have to help me dress Patsy. I couldn't find anything for her to wear."

His lips curved despite himself.

"Really?" Maddy murmured, her expression clearing. "What about that shopping trip you and Aunt Roxy went on? Surely you found something for her."

"Yes. But I want her to be pretty when I fly my kite."

"Kite?"

Roxy shifted. "I may have mentioned the kite festival the hospital puts on every year. Surely you heard about it."

"Yes, but after what happened I didn't expect to…"

Maddy's sister frowned. "Of course we're going. All of us. It's a family event. And God knows you need something to take your mind off things. I go every year, and since you live here now—and since you work at the hospital that hosts it—we have to take part in it. It'll be great."

"Who did you go with before?"

"That's something I'd rather not talk about."

Roxy set the bag of doll clothes on the ground, then bent down and scooped Chloe up with a comical roar, sending the girl into hysterical giggles.

Kaleb wanted to hand over the doll and get the hell out of there before things got deeper than they already were. But it looked as if there was no escape. Especially when Maddy stood up, putting her directly in front of him. She didn't quite meet his eyes, though. The same curl that had escaped the headband she'd had when wearing that costume spiraled down the side of her face. His finger itched to touch it again. He curled the digits into his palm instead. This woman had almost as much baggage as he did.

"How did you wind up with this crew?" She nodded at the doll in Kaleb's hands.

"They were coming into the hospital at the same time I was. Your sister wasn't sure she could find your office."

"Oh, she wasn't, was she?" One brow went up. "Exactly how many times have you been here, Roxy?"

Roxy peppered Chloe's cheek with kisses. "It's a huge building. I always get lost."

Somehow he got the idea that Maddy's sister had arrived at her destination just fine in the past. So he'd been hoodwinked. And Maddy evidently wasn't thrilled about it. Well, if Roxy had ideas about doing some matchmaking, she was out of luck. Neither he nor the pulmonologist needed her help. For one thing, he didn't want a steady relationship. For another, Maddy hadn't fared too well either in the love department. And Kaleb wasn't exactly the greatest catch on the planet. There was that baggage—lots of it. His eyes went back to Chloe. Especially when it came to little girls who reminded him of Grace.

"Is it time for lunch, Mommy?"

"Yes, it is, sweetheart. Let's find Patsy something to wear before she embarrasses Dr. McBride."

Roxy sent him a sideways glance. "I bet he's held a naked doll in his arms a time or two, haven't you, Doctor?"

Heat seeped into his face, a sensation he didn't

like. Nor was he going to touch that comment. Instead, he handed the doll to Maddy.

Chloe pointed at him. "I think he should help us find clothes for her."

"Honey, I'm sure Dr. McBride has more important things to do than help us dress Patsy."

"This *is* important."

Her sister shifted the girl on her hip. "Yes, it's very important to get a man's opinion on this one. 'Does this tutu make my…er…trunk look too spacious?'"

"Roxy." Maddy's tone held a distinct warning.

"Oh, and I saw the sign-up sheet for the kite-making contest out front and added our names to it."

"Whose names?"

"Yours and mine. It's for a good cause. The funds will go to fight childhood cancer."

Kaleb's eyes suddenly felt as if they were on fire in his head.

"Let's discuss this in my office." Maddy motioned toward the open door, mouth tight, ushering her sister and daughter through it.

Kaleb hesitated in the doorway, until he heard Chloe's plea. "Can the doctor please come too?"

Maddy stared at him. "I don't know. That's up to him."

Was it his imagination or was there a hint of pleading exasperation in her voice. Or maybe she just wanted to be rescued from her sister. Whatever it was, he found himself inching past Maddy, unable to resist tweaking that strand of hair as he went by. "You look like you could use a helping hand."

"Is it that obvious?"

"From where I stand? Yes."

Then they were all inside, and Roxy unceremoniously dumped the bag of doll clothes onto Maddy's pristine desk. He noticed the frame and laptop had been replaced with new ones.

Maddy simply shook her head. "We need to hurry, honey, or we'll be late for lunch."

It took a few minutes, but Chloe finally decided on a bikini for her doll with slide-on sandals and sunglasses. Everything was soon folded and tucked back into the bag for safekeeping.

Roxy glanced at her watch. "Darn. I forgot I have a waxing appointment. I need to get going."

Maddy remained silent. The more outrageous Roxy's comments, the harder her sister seemed to try to ignore them. Maybe Roxy was trying to keep Maddy's mind off what had happened with Matthew. Or maybe she did it to goad a response from her sister. Whatever it was, there were some things one simply couldn't unhear.

Chloe hugged her aunt goodbye and Roxy offered her hand to Kaleb, which he shook. "Nice meeting you."

"I'm sure we'll be seeing more of each other. 'Bye!"

The second the door closed behind her, Maddy sank into her chair with a sigh. "Sorry about that. Roxy has had a… Never mind. She's had a hard life."

Harder than Maddy's? Than his? That he couldn't imagine. Maybe she saw the doubt on his face, because she motioned him to a chair. "She was attacked in her home five years ago. The result was an unplanned pregnancy, which ended in a stillbirth. She uses the shock factor to keep people at a distance. It works."

Yes, it did. Kaleb did the same thing. Not through his words, but his actions. Like not sleeping at a woman's house. Like making sure he didn't sleep with the same woman more than once. In fact, it had been a while since he'd been with anyone. It was just too hard and complicated. So he didn't even try anymore.

"I'm sorry."

"Don't you dare tell her I said anything to you. She would kill me." Maddy smiled, although it looked slightly wan. "And maybe even you."

"Did they find the man who did it?"

"Yes. He's in jail." She glanced at her daughter, who was in the far corner, playing with her doll. "I think that's what's behind her fascination with costume design. She can become invisible. No one ever sees the true Roxy."

Kaleb had a couple of masks like that, but they weren't the kind that could be stitched together.

He had to ask. "Is that why you decided to wear one of her creations?"

"No. That was all my sister. I think she thought it would help me with my…with the problems I'd had with my ex in the past. But after what he did at the hospital…" Her jaw tightened. "Let's just say I've had enough secrets and hiding to last a lifetime."

Kaleb could understand that. Unfortunately, he had no desire to splay his life out for all to see. Some things were better off remaining out of sight, even if they were never really out of mind.

Glancing at her watch, Maddy sighed. "Well, I don't have that much time left for lunch. How do you feel about hospital food?"

"You mean as a patient or as a doctor?"

"I don't think there's much difference, do you?"

"No. And that sounds good to me. Do you have to take Chloe back to school?"

"She only goes half a day. Roxy will come back and get her. She normally watches her in the afternoons for me."

A few minutes later, they managed to find a table for two and squeeze another chair in for Chloe. He waited with the little girl while Maddy went up and got them something to eat. Luckily she kept up a stream of nonstop chatter, which meant Kaleb didn't have to think of anything to say. She was very excited about the whole kite-festival thing, from what he gathered. He'd never actually been back to the hospital's childhood-cancer wing since Grace's death. He'd spent enough time there to last him a lifetime.

He wasn't even sure how he'd found himself in the cafeteria with Maddy and her daughter. He'd had the perfect opportunity to leave when Roxy had. But he'd stuck around anyway. And learned something about Maddy in the process. As exasperated as she might get with her sister, she loved her fiercely. And Roxy loved her back. To the point of trying to help Maddy cope with her own heartaches. Only no two people had the same way of dealing with those kinds of situations.

"I'm hungry."

Chloe's voice pulled him from his thoughts. He shifted to look at the serving line. "Your mom is almost done, it looks like. What do you think she's going to bring you to eat?"

"Fruit cup. I always get a fruit cup, because Patsy and I love them."

So they'd eaten here before, from the sound of it. Chloe tilted her head. "Is Mommy bringing some food for you too?"

"No. But I do think the fruit cup sounds good." And just about the only edible thing on the menu. You couldn't really hurt chopped fruit.

A tray plunked down in front of them, not a piece of fruit in sight. Instead, there were chunks of cheese perched on a few lettuce leaves.

"Oh! Cheese. I love cheese!" Chloe plucked a white square and popped it in her mouth.

Kaleb smiled. So much for fan loyalty. "No fruit?"

"Shh. They were working on more, but I didn't want to hold up the line."

He glanced at the tray again. Other than the cheese and what looked like a green smoothie in a clear container, the plate was empty. "Aren't you having anything?"

"I'll just have a liquid lunch." She held up the container.

Kaleb had had a few liquid lunches after his daughter died, but they'd been amber colored and had burned like hell as they'd slid down his throat. They'd also put him down for the count. He wouldn't resurface until the following day, when his pounding head and queasy stomach reminded him that he was still very much alive. And Grace wasn't.

"I'll be right back." He levered himself from his chair and headed for the thinning line. When he got there, he asked for a pot of coffee, some sugar and three fruit cups.

The lady behind the counter glanced at him and then at the offerings on the ice in the silver buffet case. There were several plates of cheese on lettuce. A few sandwiches and the same bottles of juice that Maddy had chosen in various colors. "Wait right here." She left the register and went into the back.

He picked up a couple of the bottles before choosing one that looked orange—a color he recognized as belonging to something in the fruit family. Within seconds the woman was back with three bowls of cut-up fruit. He paid and took everything back to the table.

"They had some?" Maddy stared at his tray.

"They were just finishing them up, evidently." He passed the bowls and silverware to each of them and handed Maddy a coffee cup. "It looks like you could use something a little stronger than what's in that bottle."

"Yes, I could." She grinned at him. "But coffee will have to do."

It was good to see her smile, especially after all that had happened.

Maddy poured some of her green juice into a cup for her daughter.

"She actually likes that stuff?"

"It's really good. Have you ever tried it?"

"I normally like my salad on a plate, not in a cup."

She nudged him in the ribs with an elbow. "It's very good. And good for you."

He would take that as a warning to watch what

he said. He popped the top on his own juice and took a slug of it. Mango…and strawberries. Flavors he recognized. But, hey, if she said hers was good too, he would take her at her word.

"So you're getting roped into making a kite. Do you know anything about them?"

Grace would have loved participating in the festival. But she'd never got the chance.

"I know how to make a paper airplane. Does that count?"

He hesitated. "The entries are pretty competitive, from what I've heard. There are prizes for the best-designed kite and the highest flier."

"Really?" She took a sip of her juice. "Maybe I should have Roxy erase my name from the list, then. I don't want to disappoint anyone."

Maybe it was the thought of how much his own daughter would have enjoyed it, maybe it was the mango in his drink messing with his head, but, before he could stop them, words came tumbling out of his mouth. "I actually studied structural engineering before going into medicine. Maybe I could help."

"How?"

"Participants in the festival normally come up with a prototype—a smaller version of the actual kite—to hang over their section of the table. That way people can browse and vote on a design. That part is separate from the actual kite-flying competition."

Chloe glanced up. "I want to make a kite! A cat kite."

Maddy laughed. "A cat kite? Well, that should be a walk in the park for this design-challenged girl. Not."

"Actually, it wouldn't be that hard."

Kaleb still wasn't sure why he was offering to help. He didn't want to be at that festival or see the kids flocking to the tables, especially since those with health problems would be given passes to the front of the line. But Grace really would have loved being there. He could do it for her. And if it made Chloe happy in the process, then it benefited both him and Maddy. If he concentrated on that, maybe it would give him a modicum of peace.

"So how does your engineering experience make this 'not that hard'?"

"We still have a few weeks until the festival. We could work up a couple of prototypes, and Chloe can be our judge as far as how it appeals to kids before we make the actual kite."

The little girl's smile grew larger. "I want to be a judge too. Can I, Mommy?"

Maddy pulled in a deep breath and blew it out, ruffling the curls over her forehead. "I guess we can give it a try and see what happens."

Even as she said the words, Kaleb was having second thoughts. Was he really going to do this?

It looked that way. And seeing Chloe's excited face beaming at him and Maddy, he knew he wouldn't be able to retract the offer now. Even if he wanted to. Even if it meant facing cancer-stricken kids at that festival.

Could he do it? He wasn't sure, but he'd better figure out a way.

And he'd better do it before March first. When the kite festival officially got under way.

# CHAPTER FOUR

"I'm fine, Mom. Honest."

Maddy knew her mother would be desperately worried about her daughter's state of mind following Matthew's shocking death. Guilt sluiced up her throat every time that terrible image came back to mind. No matter how many times she heard the words *it's not your fault*, it didn't stop the ball of regret that was lodged in her belly over what had happened.

Chloe had never asked about her father, but someday she would.

And now their tiny town newspaper had blown the story up to Romeo and Juliet proportions. Only there was nothing remotely romantic about what had transpired. She hoped Chloe never read the article.

According to the press, the "beloved son"

Gamble Point had buried a week ago had been distraught, his heart so broken that he'd had no option but to end the pain. All because of the woman who'd run off to the big city, leaving him behind and taking his young daughter with her.

The facts were true enough, but they'd been so distorted that they no longer resembled reality. And they chose to pointedly ignore the fact that Matthew had endangered the lives of more people besides himself. He hadn't gone off to a lonely stretch of road and quietly killed himself. He'd terrorized an entire floor of the hospital, causing untold distress to dozens of staff and patients. One nurse had even quit her job because she was too afraid to return to work.

But small towns sometimes chose to blind themselves in an effort to protect one of their own. Maddy was allowed to say that, because she'd been born and raised in Gamble Point. She knew the town's faults. And yet she still loved the folks there. In some ways, they loved her too. But they also wanted to believe in the romantic dream.

A dream that had become one of her worst nightmares.

"You know what they printed isn't true, don't you?"

"Of course I know it's not, honey. Do you want me to come?" The worry in her mother's voice was unmistakable. But if she asked her mom to rush to Seattle, that worry would somehow transmit itself to Chloe, and Maddy had been very careful to shield her daughter from what had happened at the hospital a week and a half ago.

Besides, she was supposed to meet Kaleb at the park today to test one of the kite prototypes. Roxy was going to pick Chloe up from school and spend the afternoon with her.

Which meant she'd be alone with Kaleb for the trial run. They both agreed they didn't want Chloe disappointed if the thing didn't fly as he hoped it would. But her daughter was going to have to learn to live with disappointment. Just as Maddy had.

But not yet.

"No, Mom. I really am okay."

"You didn't come home for the funeral."

She blinked a couple of times. "Please tell me you didn't expect me to."

"No. But I kind of hoped now that Matthew is—you know—you might consider moving back to Nebraska."

Shock stopped her for several long seconds. It hadn't even occurred to her to move back home. Why? Her mom was right. There was certainly nothing stopping her now.

But she'd come to love Seattle over the last year. The busy pace of life melded with a laid-back population. And yet, the only reason she'd moved here was to get away from Matthew's threats. And the deep fear that he might try to do something to Chloe.

The guilt over her mother having to rely on other people to help her work the farm came back in a rush. Should she go?

"Maybe you should consider coming to live here, near Roxy and me. Get an apartment."

"And leave your daddy and Patricia? They're both buried here on the property, Maddy."

The plot for her sister had been placed right next to her dad's. There was no way her mom was going to leave the farm.

"Can you at least come to visit, sometime? Roxy and Chloe would both love to see you. Chloe misses her nana."

Matthew's parents had died in a car accident the year Maddy had married their son. It was just as well. It would have killed his mother—a sweet woman who wouldn't hurt a fly—to know what her son was capable of. The way things had turned out, she'd never had to witness what her son had become. Maddy's gut churned at the thought.

"I miss Chloe too. Which is why I was hoping you would come home. But I guess I understand. Our little town can't hold a candle to big-city life."

"It's not that, Mama. It's just…" She tried to think out exactly what was stopping her from going back. She found it. "There are some memories there that I'd rather not have to face on a daily basis."

"I'm so sorry, honey. If your father had been alive, he'd have never allowed things to escalate the way they did."

"It's no one's fault but mine for not leaving the second Matthew raised a hand to me."

There was a pause. "Let's not talk about that now. So what do you think? Can an old woman like me learn to fly?"

"Fly?"

"On an airplane." Her mom laughed. "Scared to death of those tin cans, actually. Maybe I'll get a bus ticket instead."

"Let me check and see how long they take to get here, Mom. Maybe I can come get you instead."

"I can manage. I've been on my own for a while now. I kind of like my independence."

"I've learned a lot from you, Mom. Okay, let me know when you're thinking of coming, and I'll carve out a spot for you to sleep."

"The couch will be fine."

"Of course it won't. You can have Chloe's bed and she can sleep with me. She'll love it."

"I'm looking forward to it. Love you, honey."

"Love you too."

Maddy smiled, happy the conversation had ended on such a good note. She'd been worried for a second or two that her mom really would try to guilt her into coming back home. But she hadn't. Maybe because Roxy had left almost as soon as she'd got out of high school. Maddy had stayed in her hometown until a year ago. But at thirty-two, it had been time, even if Matthew hadn't started getting more vocal with his threats.

And she was going to meet Kaleb to fly a kite. That shouldn't set a tiny spark of excitement jumping inside her, but it did. She wasn't sure why. As horrified as she'd been at Matthew's death, a part of her was glad she would never have to worry about him again. That could be part of the reason she was so giddy about this excursion. But she needed to curb her enthusiasm. She didn't want Kaleb thinking that she was interested in anything other than a trip to the park to check out his design.

That was all she was going to check out.

No quick glances at sundry body parts, bulges and curves either. She was going to keep all of her attention on things that were G-rated. No eyes venturing anywhere past shoulder height.

Could she do it? Oh, yes. She definitely could.

For the hundredth time, Maddy had to tear her gaze from the sight of Kaleb's haunches as he moved to adjust the altitude of his homemade kite. G-rated, huh?

Well, she'd definitely grazed something a little past PG, if not further. Worse, he'd caught her staring once, that quirky grin tossing a ball of heat right to her midsection, where it exploded and flowed to areas best left out of this whole trip.

She should have brought Chloe with her. At least her daughter would force her to keep her mind on something besides the hunky doctor. Transferring her attention to the kite, she had to admit she was impressed. That short stint in the engineering department in college had given him a head start in the kite-making department, unless that thing in the air was flying on pure dumb luck. But she didn't think so. There was no design on it at all, it was a simple cat shape, but it seemed to be flying without any trouble. So far. He'd had to tweak it a bit to the right and left a couple of times. Still, it was pretty amazing.

Kaleb glanced back. "Would you mind holding it for a few minutes? I need to make some notes on the design for the next one."

She stood, brushing a few blades of grass from her black trousers as she did. "It looks like it's doing fine."

"But it could be better."

Taking the stick wound with string, she glanced at his face. His eyes were alight with something. Excitement? Whatever it was, it was doing a number on her. "It's just an informal festival. We're not going for an international medal or anything."

"Hey, I'm just trying to make sure the thing stays in the air. I do the designing. You, Chloe and Roxy are in charge of decorating it."

Sitting on the grass, just behind her, he had

a notebook propped on one knee and was busy jotting something down. Probably those design changes he mentioned. "Funny how both mother and daughter have such a thing for cats."

"Are you talking about Jetta?"

"You were dressed like a cat when we met at the hotel, remember?"

Maddy's face flamed, and she turned around to face forward again. That was something she wasn't likely to forget anytime soon. She glanced up at the fluttering object. "Well, at least the kite didn't crash to the ground in a heap like I did."

"It didn't at that. Although you made a pretty cute heap."

He thought she was cute? Or he thought her costume was cute? There was no way she was going to ask.

"Listen." The low voice came from just over her right shoulder, causing her to start.

She cleared her throat. "Listen to what?"

"Just listen."

Maddy stared at the kite, trying to figure out exactly what she was supposed to hear. The cat above them was flittering and flapping in the stiff breeze. She could hear it as it…

"Oh, my gosh." She listened closer. Yes. The fluttering was rhythmic and low, almost like a… "Is it purring?"

"I was hoping to get something like that, which is why I put some slits in the plastic that covers the frame."

She glanced back to find he was indeed right behind her. Her eyes moistened. "Chloe is going to love this, Kaleb. Thank you so much."

"It's no problem at all."

There was a strange gleam in his eye, and when she caught sight of the notebook open on the ground, the page wasn't filled with a bunch of random scribblings about design formulas, but contained a sketch instead.

Of her. Flying his kite.

A warm tingling curled through her body. Maybe she hadn't been the only one looking. And he wasn't flipping pages to try to hide the sketch, which meant he didn't care if she saw it.

"Kaleb?"

One side of his mouth tilted up, and his fingers traced one of her cheekbones, the soft touch causing her to lose her grip on the spool of string. She fumbled for it and it hit the ground, then skittered across it with a *bump, bump, bump* as it became airborne for seconds at a time. "Oh, no!"

They both dived for the escaping spindle and ended up colliding with each other instead. Maddy chuckled, still trying to right herself so she could take off after the cord, which was rapidly unwinding, sending the kite higher and higher. She leaped for it one more time before tripping all over again. Down she went onto her hip with a thump, laughing as she rolled onto her back in the lush grass, hand to her chest. She expected Kaleb to keep sprinting after the runaway kite, but he didn't. Instead, he levered himself onto the ground beside her, leaning over her, his smile as carefree as she felt.

"It's getting away!" Her voice sounded breathless to her own ears.

"Let it."

Unlike Maddy's bright laughter, there was a

dark undertone to those two words. Her eyes met his, and she understood why, instantly. She'd felt the same thing as she'd watched him earlier: a mixture of lust and longing.

Those two emotions were mirrored in his steady gaze.

And suddenly she realized one thing: he was going to kiss her. Right here in the middle of the park.

And she wanted him to. Desperately.

Half-afraid she might be daydreaming the whole thing and that she would snap back to attention and find he was still flying the kite while she watched him from her perch on the blanket, she curled her hand around his nape and murmured his name again.

And then he was bending closer, his warm breath stirring the fine hairs on her temple.

The first touch of his lips against hers set off a chain reaction she was powerless to ignore. His elbows landed on either side of her shoulders, and he lifted his head to look at her as if trying to gauge her reaction. When he moved in again, the pressure was firmer, more insistent. Nothing like the light exploratory touch a second ago. No, his head shifted a quarter turn to the left, his mouth fitting perfectly over hers.

Settling in.

And she was okay with that. The fingers at his nape wandered to one of his shoulders, the muscles bunching deliciously under her skin. All thoughts of kites and laughter were long gone. This was deadly serious—the stuff pillow talk was made of. Only Maddy didn't feel like talking. And she hoped Kaleb didn't either.

They shouldn't be doing this. She knew it. He probably did too. The last thing she needed was to kiss a colleague. But right now, nothing would be able to pry her away. She made a sound low in her throat.

She'd wanted Chloe to be here earlier. As a buffer. Right now, though, she was glad her daughter was miles and miles away with her aunt, so she couldn't see how crazy with need this man was making her.

Maddy squirmed beneath him, her whole body

flaming to life—the heat threatening to consume her. His lips left hers, traveling sideways across her jaw until he reached her ear.

"Maddy..." He nipped her earlobe, prying another raspy sound from her. "Did you know that you purr too?"

Did she?

She had no idea, but she just might, because he was making all kinds of wonderful sensations spiral through her head. Her body. Her...

"Hey, guys, sorry to interrupt..."

The half-amused voice had not come from the person who'd been kissing her.

Horrified, Maddy jackknifed upright, knocking Kaleb off her chest in the process.

A police officer stood over them, the string from the errant kite dangling from one hand. "Missing something?"

Yes! Her good sense. She glanced over at Kaleb to see that he wasn't bothered at all. He sat up and took the item from the man. "Thank you. We did try to rescue it."

The officer made a noise that wasn't quite a

scoff, but it was close. Maybe it was just a cough. He motioned to an area a hundred yards away. "I'm afraid your kite didn't survive its landing. Nice job, though. Your design?"

"Yes. I have a few adjustments to make before it's perfect."

Maddy felt paralyzed, unable to say anything that would make any sense at this point.

"I think you might want to work on those...adjustments somewhere else," the policeman said with a smile.

Heat flamed to her cheeks and boiled up through her forehead.

Kaleb simply stood and shook his hand. "Much appreciated, and we will."

They would?

Oh, Kaleb was talking about the kite, not their make-out session.

Okay, it hadn't been a make-out session. It was just...just...

Words failed her. Because the officer had thought it was, if she wasn't mistaken. He'd basically told them—in a nice way—to move along.

More heat poured into her face. Kaleb reached down to help her up. She gladly let him, although she wasn't sure her legs were going to hold her up. She tottered to the side a step or two.

Yep. Shaky as hell.

"I'm so sorry," she started, only to have the police officer cut her off.

"Don't be. It's a beautiful place." He glanced up at the sky. "But the rain is coming. I didn't want your kite to be completely ruined, in case it can be fixed."

"Very much appreciated, Officer."

Maddy was happy for an excuse to flee. "I'll go get the kite. Thank you again."

Nodding once, the policeman headed on his way. She went after the downed kite only to find Kaleb dogging her heels, winding the string as he went.

She glanced back at him, mortified, and repeated her earlier words. "I'm so sorry."

"For what?"

"Isn't it obvious?" She trudged forward. "Kissing you. I haven't been so embarrassed in—"

"I think you have that backward, Maddy." He stopped her with a touch to her arm.

"Maybe. I guess…" She blinked. "Oh, I don't know. I just didn't expect to be rolling around on the ground with the first available man who—"

"Who said I'm available?"

For a horrific moment, she thought he was serious. Then she realized he was laughing at her, seemingly unfazed by what had happened. Well, maybe he kissed women all the time in the park.

She decided to fight fire with fire. "Maybe I'm not available either."

Which was a ridiculous thing to say. He had seen her ex-husband up close and personal.

"That bare finger on your left hand says otherwise. No recent engagements?"

Her fingers curled into her palm in an instant. But he was right. And she'd stopped wearing her wedding ring a long time ago. She chanced a peek at Kaleb's hand in case she'd missed something. She hadn't. "Yours is bare too, so I guess we're even."

"It would seem that way."

She started forward again, afraid if she didn't she might suggest they take up where they'd left off. That was one thing she definitely shouldn't do. She didn't need the complication. And neither did Kaleb. Nor did her daughter, who had been uprooted from her home and dragged three states away from everything she'd known and loved.

Only Chloe seemed to love Seattle just as much as Maddy did.

"Well, this is not going to happen again." Reaching the kite, she grabbed it. The police officer was right about its condition. The poor thing's wooden skeleton was broken in four places. One of those, a compound fracture, had the stick coming right through the plastic skin.

"And you're sure of this why?"

Was he kidding? There was no way he should want this any more than she should.

Except she had. And she did. Definitely not a good combination. "Because I have a daughter, and I don't want her to get hurt."

That seemed to bring Kaleb to his senses. In fact, his face seemed to pale slightly. "Right.

No parent wants to see their child get hurt. Or suffer."

There was something in his words that made her pause and blink up at him before her gaze moved lower. His left ring finger was bare, just as hers was. But like hers, it was hard to completely erase an indentation where a ring once was. And Kaleb's finger had a definite depression across the base of the digit, although the skin stretched across it was as tanned as the rest of his finger. So it had been a while.

Had he had a child? A wife? If so, where were they?

Before she could even form a question, Kaleb had taken the kite from her hands and turned it over in his own. "Speaking of kids, I'd better get this back to my place and fixed up. Or you will have one disappointed child on your hands." His jaw tightened slightly. "And as for what happened a few minutes ago, I agree with you. It is not going to happen again. I'll make sure of it."

Kaleb paused with the suture material still in his hand—his patient sitting with his lacerated chin

tilted toward him. How could he have let himself get so carried away yesterday at the park?
He'd been oblivious to everything around him—
even the police officer—totally caught up in kissing Maddy. He hadn't done something like that
since…

Since he and Janice had met in medical school.
That first semester had been a blur of getting to
know each other. Moving in together. Getting
married.

Having a child.

They'd waited to get pregnant until they'd both
graduated, so they would have time to spend with
their child. He hadn't realized how little of that
there would be, in the end. If only he'd been more
attuned to what was happening with Grace, he
could have…

He stifled the thought, poking the needle
through the next section of tissue, and tried to
make sense of what had happened at the park.

This weird urge to sketch Maddy had come
over him as he'd watched her wrestle with that
length of line on the kite. And of course sketching

meant looking. And when his gaze had drifted down her body, his own flesh had been busy tightening. His mind had already been traveling down dangerous paths at the speed of light. And when she'd noticed the purring sound he'd worked so hard to perfect, and had recognized it for what it was, it had sent a jagged bolt of sensation arching through his gut—the ill-concealed wonder in her eyes doing a number on him.

When he'd actually bent to kiss her, he'd only meant it to be a quick peck and release. Just enough to whet his appetite but not enough to actually satisfy it. Only once he'd started, he hadn't been able to stop. Until that officer had made him think past his belt buckle.

Then she'd mentioned her daughter, and sent his thoughts reeling to another place and time. That was when he'd really started wondering what the hell he'd been thinking.

He still wasn't sure.

"Are you okay, Mr. Jansen?" His patient, a fifty-two-year-old man, had decided to cannonball into his swimming pool and wound up smacking his chin against the hard concrete side. He should have been old enough to know better.

But then again, so should Kaleb. Kissing a woman with a child was one of his unspoken rules. He didn't get involved with anyone who had little kids. Then again, he didn't get involved with women at all, with or without children.

And he'd better damn well remember that.

"I'm okay." His patient's words were slurred. Not because of alcohol consumption—although Kaleb could bet good old Mr. Jansen had had at least a couple of beers—but because of the local anesthetic he'd been given. All this to impress a woman.

Hadn't Kaleb tried to do the same thing with that kite? Purring, his ass. What was wrong with him? He should have just made a triangular two-stick kite like every other dad on the planet.

Dad?

Oh, hell. There was something very wrong with him. There had to be.

"Just a few more stitches, and we'll be done."

"Will it scar?"

Absolutely. Just like every other spot on the human body that split open.

Like his heart?

Yes, but that had happened far too long ago. He should not be flinching every time he saw a child—interacted with one. Helped build a kite with one.

The stitches that closed his own emotional cut had been removed long ago, the wound sealed tight against all invaders. But the scar was still there. Still sensitive to the slightest touch. Somehow he needed to figure out a way to deaden it, just as he'd numbed his patient's chin.

Easier said than done. He reacted every time he heard about or saw Chloe Grimes—that old familiar ache making itself known.

She looked nothing like Grace. His own daughter's hair had been dark brown and her personality had been nothing like Chloe's, but Maddy's little girl still affected him on a gut level. And he wasn't sure how to make it stop.

Or how to make his attraction for her mother go away. Nothing good could come of any of this.

For either him or Maddy. So he needed to just let it go—pull back and keep his distance from both her and her daughter. That wasn't an option as long as the kite festival was under way. But once it was over, he was going to cut himself loose and fly away—just like his runaway kite.

No matter how difficult that might turn out to be.

# CHAPTER FIVE

"WE ARE GRATEFUL to all of our staff who have agreed to participate in next week's event." The hospital CEO's voice had a soothing quality to it. So much so that it was beginning to lull Maddy to sleep. She jammed her fist beneath her chin and pushed down hard to help chase away the feeling. "The winner of the best-kite award will receive tickets for four to the city's Space Needle and a voucher to dine in the restaurant."

That perked her up. Chloe would love going up to the observation platform. Her daughter had always been an adventurer, climbing, running, jumping. So much so that a year ago, she'd somehow found her way to the top of the refrigerator, much to Maddy's horror. A stern talking-to hadn't even fazed the little girl. And since the kite festival fell on her own birthday, it would be the perfect way to celebrate.

She chanced a glance at Kaleb, who was sitting two rows to the left of her in the hospital's large assembly room, which served not only as a staffing area in case of a city-wide emergency, but also a convenient place to hold meetings. Not everyone could attend at once, for obvious reasons, but the informational gatherings were taped so that staff who were on duty would know what was discussed.

Kaleb was looking at Dr. Druthers as if fascinated by every word that came out of the man's mouth. She wasn't fooled, though. She'd caught his attention shifting toward her more than once.

He had to regret this whole kite-making fiasco. She hadn't talked to him since that day in the park almost a week ago, but she had seen him from time to time in the hospital corridors or striding back and forth between their building and the hotel. She'd forced herself to stay busy so she didn't stare out of her office window at the road below. Still, she'd noticed him walking across the street toward the hospital more than once as his shift was ending. Watching for him had become almost a ritual. One she didn't like, but couldn't seem to break.

Before Maddy had time to avert her eyes, his head swung slightly to the right, and he caught her gaze. Again. This time one side of his mouth went up in that crazy sexy smile that made her squirm inside. She didn't want to react. Tried to school her features into a completely neutral mask. But the corners of her own lips tipped. And not down, either. Nope, they went up as surely as that kite Kaleb had made.

She should be avoiding the man like the plague. And she'd tried to. It was obvious they were going to have to communicate on some level, because this kite was for Chloe. He was designing it, but surely he expected the little girl's help in decorating it. Her smile widened slightly at that thought. She hoped the man liked froufrou, because her daughter loved ribbons and pastel colors.

But he was going to make it purr. She could not wait to see Chloe's face when the little girl

heard it. Her eyes stung, blurring her vision a little bit. And she couldn't stop herself from mouth-
ing "Thank you" to the man who was going to
make her daughter a very happy girl. On Maddy's birthday, no less.

His smile faded, his response a curt nod.

Maddy's eyes widened. What was that all
about?

Dr. Druthers started getting into the particu-
lars about how the yearly festival at Fountain
Park was going to benefit the hospital. The children's cancer wing would be receiving the bulk
of the incoming donations. The man motioned to
someone and the lights went dim. On the screen
toward the front of the room, images of children appeared one by one. Children who'd been
through the cancer ward. The kids were in various stages of disease. Some had their hair. Some
didn't. Some were clutching stuffed animals or
hugging Embry the Clown, the official mascot of
the wing. Her eyes sought out Kaleb again, only
he was no longer looking at her. Nor was his at-

tention focused on the presentation. He was staring down at the floor instead.

Weird. She could understand doing that when the speech was going on. It had been rather dry. But to not look at the difference the festival was going to make in the lives of some very special children? That seemed rather callous.

Maybe he was just tired. Or maybe the sight of the kids in their "battle gear"—consisting of bald heads and IV ports—made him uncomfortable. She knew it did her. But she liked to put faces to the cancer fight. It made working with Kaleb worth all of the discomfort. Surely they could survive each other's company for another week until this was all over with? Especially for a cause like this one.

A few minutes later, the slide show was over, and the lights came back up. But when she looked to see if Kaleb was still gazing at his shoes, the concierge doctor was nowhere to be seen. He'd evidently slipped out sometime between the discussion of childhood brain tumors and leukemia. Oh, well, it didn't matter. She'd been inspired, even if Kaleb hadn't. If he couldn't bring himself to do his damnedest for the kids on that screen, then Maddy would have to have enough enthusiasm for the both of them.

When the meeting was over, she was one of the first people out of the room. She rounded the corner to find Kaleb standing over by the nurses' desk, making small talk with a blonde bombshell. So that was why he'd left. He probably had a date with her and came out to close the deal. Only he wasn't wearing his normal flirtatious grin. He'd sent Maddy more meaningful glances than he was giving that woman. Then the nurse came around the desk and caught him up in a hug.

Shock rolled through her system. Followed by disbelief.

Well, great. She wasn't going to stand here and watch him pick up someone to pass the night with. Although the fact that he could kiss her as he had less than a week ago and then jump into the arms of another woman was a kick to her ego. He'd said there would be no more kissing between them, and he certainly seemed anxious to stick to his side of that bargain.

Well, fine.

She forced herself to walk past the desk, unable to watch them a second longer. When she got to the elevator, though, he was right behind her. She ignored him, stepping into the car with ten other passengers—all leaving the meeting. When he moved to stand next to her, she made it a point to stare at the numbers overhead. If she could just get through three more floors, she would get off and Kaleb would continue on his way down. And she wouldn't have to see that damned hug replaying through her skull time and time again.

Her floor came and off she got. She pulled in a deep breath and was just getting ready to let it hiss back through her teeth when something touched her arm.

"Can I talk to you for a minute?"

Was he kidding? Had the blonde turned him down or something? Well, if he expected her to step into the woman's shoes, he was going to be sorely disappointed. "Of course. About what?"

"I know this competition thing could get awkward, and I thought we should clear the air."

Oh…he was not! "Competition? I'm not competing with anyone."

"Yes, you are. The kite festival?"

It took her a second to change tracks. "Oh. The kite festival. Of course."

"What did you think I was talking about?"

Wow, she really was an idiot. And a pitiful one at that.

"It's not important."

"I would like to do good by Chloe for that contest—make the best kite we can." He paused. "Unless you think the Space Needle isn't something she would be interested in."

Her icy heart thawed. "It would be the highlight of her year. Do you really think you can pull off winning?"

"No."

The wind went right out of her sails. "Oh, of course, I don't expect you to—"

His hand came out as if he was going to brush a strand of hair out of her face, but he put it back down. "I don't want to win it on my own. I've been thinking. I really want Chloe to feel she's had a part in making the kite. It would make me feel...I would like *her* to feel included. Are you okay with that?"

"Of course. Why wouldn't I be?"

"Well, after that business at the park, I wondered if..." He paused again. "If you'd tell me to forget the whole thing."

If she were smart, she might do exactly that, but Chloe was looking forward to working with Kaleb on it. "It doesn't matter what I want or don't want. Chloe would be devastated if I tried to keep her from that kite. I told her about it purring, and she can't wait to hear it for herself. And to see it fly. So, yes, I'm happy to keep working together, until the festival is done. Then we can go our separate ways."

"I'll try not to make it any more uncomfortable than it has to be."

"I've been uncomfortable before and survived with barely a nick."

Well, that wasn't exactly true. Matthew had

given her more than one nick. Some worse than others. No, this would be nothing compared to that. And if she could make it through the stuff in her past, she could make it through anything.

Kaleb studied her for a moment or two. "I think you have. Survived, that is."

"We all have, or we wouldn't be here." She shook her head. "What do you want Chloe and me to do?"

"I want to know what her favorite colors are. And to know if we're going for a realistic representation of a cat or an abstract fun version. Can you ask your daughter which she'd prefer?"

"I can already tell you that. She adores Jetta. She would probably love it if the kite could look very similar to him. Right down to his different-colored eyes."

"I didn't notice the cat having two different eyes."

"Really? Most people see it right away. He has one bright green and one amber."

"My mind wasn't exactly on your cat's eyes."

That sardonic sense of humor was back in full force.

Well, she wasn't going to touch that last comment. Not if she knew what was good for her. Although that was debatable at the moment. "Well, they're one of his best features."

"I thought his best feature was his purr. It was loud. Really loud."

"Jetta does have quite a motor on him. Is that why you decided to make the kite version of him purr?"

"It seemed fitting. Although if Chloe had decided on a unicorn cat, I was going to have a little trouble figuring out that aspect of it."

"I'll ask her, just to make sure, but I'm pretty sure she would love having Jetta immortalized in kite form. Without the horn."

"You got it." He pushed the button to get back into the elevator. It was then that she noticed her department was bustling just as much as it normally was with nurses running here and there as they went about their tasks. It was strange that she hadn't been aware of any of that until just now. No, she'd only had eyes for the man with the kite. And it looked as if he was aiming to win.

He already had, as far as she was concerned. That worried her. But she could think about that later.

"Thank you again, Kaleb, for doing this for her."

"My pleasure." This time when his hand came out, he didn't stop midmotion. Instead, he pressed his fingers to hers for several seconds until the elevator door dinged its arrival. Only then did he move away. But the feel of his skin against hers followed her long after the doors had closed behind him.

Kaleb woke with a start. Staring up at the dark ceiling, he tried to figure out where he was. His room.

He untangled himself from the sheets and hung his legs over the side of the bed, propping himself up with his hands. He was drenched in sweat.

Again.

Dammit.

He dragged shaky fingers through his hair, trying to slow his breathing.

Those dreams were now following him from sleep to sleep. He shifted his head from one side to the other, letting the crack of his cervical vertebrae anchor him back to reality.

His daughter was not trapped in a bottomless well. Nor had he been trying everything in his power to reach her: ropes, life preservers, scaling the walls with his bare hands. He lifted his fingers to look at them. No bloody stumps.

"It was a dream."

A never-ending nightmare was more like it.

Because the reality was that Grace had never been trapped in a well. Instead the vision always morphed to something closer to reality. His daughter, splayed on a hospital bed, her face paler than pale. Only in his dream, he reached for her chart to see what treatment her doctors recommended only to find the first page stamped with the words *Too Late*. As was the next. Page after page held the same terrible phrase. He flipped faster and faster, looking for some sign of hope.

There had to be something. Something the doctors—something that *he*—could do. Panic engulfed him, along with a horrible premonition. He slowly turned back toward the bed.

This was where he'd woken up each night. With the horror that it was no longer Grace's lifeless form lying on that bed, but Chloe's. And on the other side of her was Maddy. And in her face an accusation he'd lobbed at himself.

*Too Late.*

Hell! He climbed out of bed and pulled on a pair of sweatpants. Maybe if he burned some calories, he'd feel better. But thirty minutes in his weight room only left him tired and sweaty. It did nothing to erase what he'd seen in his dream.

Grace had been dead for five years. He hadn't had nightmares about her in ages. Was it because of Chloe and Maddy? Were they dredging up old regrets and flaying them open all over again?

Chloe was a normal healthy girl. She and Grace had nothing in common. Not their age, not their appearance.

Going into his drawing room, he sat at the

drafting table to look at the designs for the kite. It was almost done. Almost ready for Chloe and Maddy to come over and…

Was that what it was? He was worried about them coming into his space and upsetting his equilibrium?

It was much more likely that Maddy would do that than Chloe. She'd already upset him in more ways than one.

Like that kiss? The one he couldn't seem to forget?

Why couldn't he dream about that? About laying her softly down on his bed and…

Dammit. This was no better than his nightmares. Yes, actually it was. Because at least this was something he could comprehend. The man-wants-woman thing was much easier to understand and accept.

All of a sudden, being a winner didn't sound like such a great idea.

He pushed the kite a little to the left on the table. Maybe he should purposely sabotage the design and lose. Handing Maddy a promise that they could win the prize wasn't one of his brighter decisions. Because if they won, Kaleb would not get to walk away as he'd told himself a few minutes ago. Winning had consequences. Like the trip up the Space Needle. He could tell Maddy to give his ticket to someone else. But then he'd have to explain why he didn't want to go. A talk he didn't want to have. Not with her. Not with anyone on the committee who might also wonder.

And Roxy, Maddy's sister, who'd asked him to figure out if she could add fur to a kite and still get lift off, or if it would be too heavy to move.

Kind of like Kaleb's life nowadays.

He sighed and pushed back from the table.

Maybe he was going about this all wrong. Maybe he shouldn't be trying to avoid the inevitable. He was attracted to Maddy, and he was pretty sure from that kiss that the attraction was mutual. If he couldn't get her out of his head one way, maybe he should go at it from a completely different angle. How about if he approached it as he did any other woman? Spend a quick night together at his place. Maybe then he could walk away from that night the way he always did. No strings. No promises. Just a single night of pleasure.

His gut churned at the thought. Maddy wasn't like all those other women. And for years, he'd avoided being with women who had children.

Could it be that that tactic had backfired, though? Had made him dig a rut that just got deeper and deeper with each new person?

He had no idea. But maybe it was time to test that theory. And working together with Maddy gave him the perfect opportunity to do just that: see if he could get past this particular roadblock. And he could think of no person he'd rather experiment with than her.

Kaleb yawned, the muscles in his body finally relaxing, probably wondering what had taken him so long to figure this whole thing out.

*Well, tough luck, buddy. You wanted to wake me up, well, now you can just stay awake. Because we have a kite-making contest to enter. And to win.*

\* \* \*

Chloe pasted the last of the glittery claw stickers onto the body of the kite. Maddy had to admit her sister had done a great job painting the kite, solid black with various areas of shadow and light. Kaleb had warned them against adding too many layers of color to the kite, saying it would make it too heavy. She was amazed. He'd calculated the weight down to the gram, had even weighed the faux claws and the two custom eye stickers—one green and one amber—that Roxy had designed herself. They'd made the smaller demo model that would hang over their table look identical. Only it wouldn't need to fly.

This one did.

They wouldn't get a chance to test it, as they had its prototype. She would have to trust that Kaleb had got it right. Besides, if they tried and it crashed and burned as the last one had, they wouldn't have time to start over.

That disastrous flight hadn't been Kaleb's fault. It had been hers for letting go of the string.

But the result of her goof up? Well, that had

been pretty spectacular. She could only thank her lucky stars that a police officer had retrieved the string and set her and Kaleb back on their feet.

But watching him as he painstakingly checked the new kite after each addition, she had to admit he was pretty damned hot. And not just in the looks department. He'd been kind to Chloe, even as he looked uncomfortable whenever he had to work directly with her.

Some men just didn't like children.

But he'd been married. So what had happened between him and his wife? Had they disagreed over whether or not to have kids?

Or maybe they'd had some and Kaleb, for whatever reason, hadn't got visitation rights. He'd never mentioned having children, though.

Kaleb picked up a foam roller and went over each of the claw stickers one by one, making sure they were tightly adhered to the body of the kite.

"Did you really make the last one purr?" Roxy asked.

He sent her a quick grin. "I know right where the purr buttons are, so yes."

Out of the corner of her eye, she saw her sister's eyebrows shoot up. Roxy jabbed a thumb toward Chloe. "Little pitchers, big ears."

"I'm talking about the kite, Roxy. Those cut-outs you grumbled about earlier? They'll vibrate in the wind and make a kind of purring sound."

When she looked skeptical, Maddy pointed out one of the gill-like slits that lined the cat's torso. "It works. I heard it when we flew the unpainted version."

Kaleb nodded. "It's one of the reasons the paint had to be lighter in those areas. The plastic has to be able to flutter in order to make the sound."

"Well, I'll be." Her sister looked at the kite again.

Chloe's feet got dangerously close to the edge of the chair as she tried to see what they were talking about. Kaleb scooped her up, one arm under the backs of her legs, making her squeal with laughter before he turned her so she had a clear view of Jetta's twin. "Pretty, pretty kitty!" she declared.

Maybe the purring was overkill. Chloe seemed

more taken with the way the kite looked than with its functionality. Maybe if it survived its maiden flight, Maddy could buy it off Kaleb and put it on her daughter's wall. A sweet memory of a fun event.

These were the kinds of memories normal fathers made with their children.

Maddy gritted her teeth. Kaleb was not Chloe's father, and he never would be. She needed to get that notion out of her head immediately. Not that it had ever been there in the first place, but she needed to be careful. Chloe had taken a liking to this man. So had Roxy.

So had she. It was time to dial back on the Dr. McBride fan club. She held out her arms for her daughter, only to have Chloe nestle closer to Kaleb's chest, wrapping her tiny arms around his neck.

Maybe he sensed her unease, because he knelt on the floor next to the table. "What do you say we go to work on Roxy's kite next? We still have some more fur to glue to it."

This time her daughter willingly let go of him. "Can I help glue?"

Roxy stepped forward and took Chloe by the hand. "Oh, most definitely. We're about to make ourselves a flying unicorn. How does that sound?"

"Not too much glue," Kaleb warned. But when he acted as if he was going to follow them, Maddy touched his arm.

"Hey. Can I talk to you for a minute?"

He tucked his fingers into the pockets of his jeans, hooking his thumbs over the tops of them. "Sure. What's up?"

Now that she had made her mind up to say something, she wondered if she was doing the right thing. She glanced over to where her daughter and Roxy were busy working. "Chloe is young…and…" Taking a deep breath, she tossed the rest of the sentence out before she could back out. "She seems to be developing a tiny bit of a crush on you. If you could keep that in mind when you're around her, I would appreciate it."

His eyes narrowed slightly. "As in you want me to watch my p's and q's."

"Or maybe maintain a little distance between you and her."

"Between me and her." His head tilted. "And what about you? Should I keep my distance there as well?"

Maddy's mouth watered. That hadn't been exactly what she'd been trying to say. "I'm a big girl. I think I can handle myself."

"Can you?"

Okay, the man was playing word games, and she had no idea what he meant by that. But if he wanted to lob a few serves her way, she could match him stroke for stroke. "You can bet on it."

"I might like to take you up on that wager." Rubbing his chin with his thumb, he paused, something dark flashing in his eyes. But before she could look closer, it winked back out.

"Don't worry, Maddy. I'll keep my distance from your daughter." He took a step closer, reaching out to take a strand of her hair and sliding it over her temple. "But I have no intention of keeping my distance from you."

# CHAPTER SIX

FOUNTAIN PARK WAS awash with people on the big day. There were kites of every shape and size imaginable.

Kites weren't the only things being celebrated today, it would seem.

"Why didn't you tell me it's your birthday?"

Kaleb had overheard Roxy offer to take Chloe off her hands, so she could go home and celebrate by soaking in a hot tub.

"I'm trying to forget I'm another year older."

Older? The woman was stunning. And right now, he was trying to keep his eyes on Maddy's sister, as she tugged the string to her kite, and off the birthday girl and the image of her naked in a sea of frothy white bubbles.

Roxy's kite made it off the ground and hung suspended for a minute or two. Suddenly, it began to spiral out of control, plummeting to the ground in the strong wind.

"I warned her about that glue and using too much fur," he muttered as it crashed and burned—the first casualty of the day. Luckily for Roxy, though, all the kites' prototypes were on display in the gathering tent, including her furry unicorn. It made sense, because once the kites were sent into the air, anything could happen. Including smashing into dozens of pieces. And since Roxy's looked as if it had exploded on contact, it was a good thing.

"I can't believe it crashed so soon. Is ours going to do that?"

"It shouldn't." He said it with as much conviction as he could muster, but kite-flying was more an art than a science. There could be a defect that avoided detection, even in the most flawlessly executed design. Even in the most beautiful creation.

Like the human body. His daughter had been a prime example of that.

"Oh, well." Maddy settled into a lawn chair on

the grassy area surrounding them. "Roxy said she handed out most of her business cards to people who came by to look at the kites. She said even if hers didn't make it into the air, the effort had been well worth it. And at least she got it up."

He brought his mind back to the present. "Are you doing anything special for your birthday? Other than a night at home alone?"

"Alone?" She glanced at him with a tilt of her head. "You make it sound like a bad thing. It's not, you know. Sometimes it's a luxury."

Not always. Not when you'd gone from having a healthy, active daughter and a happy marriage to being alone. Every day. Every night.

Roxy came over moaning in despair, her poor tattered kite wilting in her hands. "It's definitely ruined. Maybe you two will have better luck."

The kites were sent into the air according to assigned numbers. It didn't matter if the entrant's kite stayed up for hours and hours, but it had to go up and be stable for at least five minutes to be considered in the running for the grand prize. They still had another ten minutes before they were set to launch their cat. Chloe was bursting with excitement, jumping up and down.

Roxy held out her hand. "Let's go get a snow cone and burn off some of that energy until it's time."

"Jetta isn't going up without us, is he?" Chloe gave her aunt a dubious glance.

"We'll be back in plenty of time." She shot Maddy a look. "You don't mind, do you?"

"Mind?" She settled deeper into her chair. "I'll just sit here and figure out what the city looks like from the Space Needle. Because we're going to… Go! Fight! Win!"

Kaleb couldn't hold back a chuckle at the impromptu cheer. He had to admit, he liked seeing Maddy and her daughter this enthusiastic about the kite. He hadn't felt this amalgamation of anticipation and dread in a long time. Probably not since Janice had left him.

No. It would have been before Grace died. Because since then his life had been consumed with more dread than anticipation. Dreading sleep. Dreading wandering into the pediatric oncology wing—even when Brenda Marlin had spotted him in the hallway as he was coming out from the meeting and hugged him last week. He'd thought of transferring hospitals to get away from those memories, but by staying here, he felt he still had some type of connection with his daughter. His ex-wife, on the other hand, had wanted to move away immediately after Grace's death. One of the things they'd clashed about during that last year. And then she'd cheated, and he'd been left totally alone.

"We've got about five minutes left. Is there anything we need to do to get ready?" Maddy's voice forced him from his thoughts.

He focused on her bright, shining face. This was the example Kaleb should follow. Despite everything that had happened with her ex-husband and that vicious attack, she'd maintained an inner glow that was undimmed.

Then again, she hadn't lost a child.

He stopped himself right there. She'd lost a husband. But from what he'd seen, the man had been a bastard.

How could anyone have wanted to hurt this woman?

Not him. In fact, he was enjoying being here with her today. Maybe a little too much.

And when the day was over?

Kaleb didn't want it to end. A thought came to him. It was her birthday. The perfect opportunity to prolong their time together. Not a wise choice, maybe, but it seemed a shame to let her go home to an empty house, despite her earlier words. It could be wishful thinking, but surely as a single parent she looked forward to indulging in adult conversation from time to time?

His mind put a subtle emphasis on the word *adult*. An emphasis he carefully ignored. He focused on her question instead.

"We should be good to go." He checked the rope sitting in its holder. "Do you want to let your sister know we're just about ready?"

"I just did." She held up her phone, and even now Roxy and Chloe were waving in the distance, snow cones in hand.

He was going to take her words about keeping

his distance from Chloe to heart. But he'd also told her he had no intention of keeping his distance from her. With her hair pulled back from her face with a headband, snug jeans and a shoulder-baring tank top, he could barely keep his eyes off her. They kept taking little sips of the view and coming back for more. It went to his head as surely as a fifth of whiskey. Smooth to the senses. But like whiskey, it could trap him in its grip almost before he realized what was happening. Which was probably why the next words came out.

"Why don't you let me take you out for your birthday? We can get something to eat."

Before she could reply, Roxy—who'd lifted Chloe onto her hip at some point—reached them.

Maddy shook her head. "She's too heavy to be carried like that."

Roxy put the girl down, wagging her finger at the child. "I told you you'd get me in trouble."

"I did not. You said you wanted to carry me. Said it was safer if you did." She took a loud slurp of the icy liquid in her snow cone, her grin infectious.

Roxy's face colored, and she blinked as if her persona of carefree hipster had just been single-handedly obliterated. "Well, it's true, you little stinker. Safer for *me*." She tickled the girl's ribs until she squealed.

A man with a clipboard stopped in front of them, glancing at the tag at the kite on the ground and writing something down. "You folks ready for the big send-off?"

"Yippee!" Chloe punched her small fist into the air. "Are we ever! We're going to win. Right, Kaleb?"

Maddy frowned. "Dr. McBride, Chloe."

He started to say it was okay for her to call him by his first name, but there was a slight tightening of Maddy's lips that warned him not to contradict her. She was right. Chloe was her daughter. Not his. He had no right to give his opinion one way or the other. About anything.

Except maybe this kite, which the judge was waiting for them to launch.

He started to take Chloe's hand and then had second thoughts. Glancing at Maddy, he asked, "Can she help me?"

Her teeth came down on her lower lip for a second before she gave a quick nod.

Chloe gave a couple of sideways hops, clapping her hands. "Yes!"

The judge gave a few last-minute instructions. Kaleb was allowed to take a running start to get the kite up, letting out the string as he went. But the kite had to stay in the air for five minutes, while the judge watched. If it passed the test, the kite was entered into the final drawing. Unfortunately, Roxy's unicorn hadn't made the cut. But he had high hopes for this one.

Several bystanders came over to watch.

Kaleb turned to Chloe. "You wait here for me. I'm going down the hill, and then I'll run back toward you. When I get here, I'll hand you the string and you can help me keep it up."

"Are you sure that's wise?" Maddy still seemed a little agitated. He wasn't sure if she was regretting letting Chloe help him or if she was worried about the kite falling from the sky prematurely. Maybe it had to do with that whole attachment thing she'd mentioned earlier.

Well, since he wasn't planning on being a permanent fixture in their lives, it didn't really matter. There was no way Chloe could actually get attached to him since she wouldn't be seeing much of him after today.

Unless the kite won. But even then, he could give his ticket to them and let them choose someone else to go with them to the Space Needle. Probably not a hard prospect. Both Maddy and her sister were beautiful. Although the man in him recognized Roxy's charm and good looks, she didn't send his blood pressure skyrocketing as Maddy did. Probably not a good thing for him to admit.

Ignoring those thoughts, he glanced at the woman herself. She crossed her fingers, gave the digits a quick kiss and held them up. Wishing him luck.

He was going to need it. Because his heart had almost convinced his head to re-ask the question about having dinner with him once this whole thing was over.

But for now, down the hill he went, checking the kite as he went. The girls had done a wonderful job decorating it. The black paint even had little brushstrokes that made it look like fur. And those mismatched eyes Roxy had glued gave the illusion of following you.

He reached the spot he'd chosen, holding the kite right next to his body. He checked the tail—black, of course—which was made to resemble the puffed-up tail of an agitated cat. Then he double-checked the structure itself. Remembering Maddy's good-luck gesture, he tossed the kite into the stiff breeze and began jogging up the hill, letting the string out as he went.

The kite caught the wind perfectly, just as he'd hoped it would do, edging higher and higher, those glittery black claws catching the sun and reflecting back at him.

It was going to work. He could tell by the way it swayed gently back and forth as it ascended.

It wasn't the jerky sawing motions of an unbalanced kite. It was almost going up too well.

He had a little girl to impress, so he crossed his own fingers, trying not to think of his daughter, as he scaled back his jog and then finally slowed to a walk. He reached the gathering crowd, which clapped to encourage them. You would have thought this was their kite and not his, Maddy's and Chloe's.

The judge glanced down at his watch. "You've just passed the one-minute mark. Four more to go."

The kite dipped for a second, but Kaleb gave it a couple of quick tugs, keeping some play in the rope as he tried to find the perfect altitude.

"Can I hold the string?" Chloe's question was a reminder that this was not just about him.

Maddy, now out of her chair, took hold of Chloe's hand. "Let him get it where he wants it first, okay?"

He was still busy trying to make sure they didn't lose before they even got started. Yes, the kite was judged by looks primarily, but the ease of getting it in the air and keeping it there was bound to have some influence over the voting members of the crowd. Someone pointed up at the kite. "It looks great. Almost real."

Oh, but they hadn't seen the best part. And they wouldn't unless he could get it facing the wind in just the right way. He was aware of Chloe's impatience as he edged the kite one way and then the other. If he could just get it to…

There.

He saw it before he heard it, those slits catching the wind and beginning to flutter.

It took a minute. Then someone said, "What's that? I hear something."

Maddy picked up Chloe, putting paid to the idea that she wasn't supposed to be carried. Then the little girl sent up a whoop that took him by surprise. "He's doing it, Mama! Jetta is purring!"

A young man standing close enough to hear Chloe's words jerked his head around to look up at the kite. "I thought I recognized that sound. Awesome!"

The words spread through the group and

phones came out to take pictures and videos of the kite. More people gathered.

"Two minutes."

Time was dragging. But that was okay. Chloe was staring up in rapt silence, probably unable to believe that their creation was in the air. And purring. She probably wasn't even aware of the reaction of the people around them. Kaleb didn't much care either. What he did care about were the mother and daughter gazing toward the heavens. He'd made this happen. And suddenly, Kaleb was damned glad he'd put the time and effort into that kite. Those endless hours of calculations and planning now seemed worth it.

Grace would have loved this.

"Four minutes."

Only one minute left. And Jetta the cat was still holding his own, his tail swishing back and forth in the sky. Who said black cats brought bad luck? This looked like one lucky feline.

"Five minutes." The judge reached out and shook Kaleb's hand and then held it out to Chloe. "Did you help decorate that cat, young lady?"

The little girl nodded.

"Well, you've done an excellent job. Congratulations."

"Thank you, sir." You would have thought the judge had already awarded her the prize from Chloe's expression. She was in awe of the official and just as in awe of the kite they'd put in the air.

"Would you like to hold it now, Chloe?" Kaleb offered her the spindle of string. She took it in both hands, holding it just as he showed her.

Roxy came over. "That was a really nice thing you did. It means a lot to Chloe. To both of them."

"It was nothing."

The woman smiled. "It most definitely was not nothing. And I won't forget it."

He had no idea what she meant by that, but he'd evidently won her approval. For some reason, he got the impression that if Roxy didn't like someone, it would be all over for that person as far as getting close to Maddy went. Roxy was protective. Because of what had happened to her? Or because of Maddy's late husband?

Either way, he was glad of it. Glad that Roxy

was taking it upon herself to make sure that Maddy didn't get involved with any more men like her ex.

Just then he heard a scream in the distance. At first he thought it was someone laughing at one of the kites. There were about fifteen of them in the air at this point, spaced far enough apart that they couldn't get tangled up with each other. The hospital had figured they would get about fifty to a hundred kite entries and, from what Kaleb could see, they were probably going to get close to the top figure. There were five judges working to get the kites launched and, so far, they'd had about an equal number go up as they had ones that crashed and burned, like Roxy's.

The scream rang out again. This time sounding a little more urgent. He glanced at Chloe to see that she was still holding the string like a pro. At this point, unless something happened to the steady breeze, she wouldn't have to work to keep it up there. It would continue flying until they brought it down. He'd pounded a holder into the grass so they could drop the string caddy into it and be able to watch the kite without having to manage it the entire time.

He caught Maddy's eye. She'd heard the sound as well. "Is somebody hurt?"

"I don't know." Using his hand to shade his eyes, he tried to look through the crowd, but couldn't see anything.

Another shout went up. This one a man's voice. Kaleb didn't like it. "I'm going to check it out."

"I'm going with you." Maddy turned to her sister. "Can you watch her? If someone's having a medical emergency, I might be able to help."

Though a lot of the hospital staff were at Fountain Park enjoying their day, he wasn't taking any chances.

"Of course." Roxy laid her hand on her niece's shoulder. "Let's sit down on the blanket so we can watch Jetta in action. Do you want me to hold the string?"

"No. I want to."

With one last glance at the pair, he and Maddy headed in the direction of the distressed calls.

* * *

Maddy didn't like the look of that crowd. In fact, she knew she didn't. Breaking into a sprint, she noted that Kaleb had had the same reaction and had outpaced her by a good ten yards. Damn, she knew she should have taken up running.

He pushed through the crowd a few seconds later and was lost to her sight. Just a couple more yards and she would be able to…

That was when she saw it. One of the golf carts that had been cruising around the park had overturned. How that had happened, she didn't have a clue. But sticking out from beneath the undercarriage of the vehicle was a pair of feet. Oh, God, the cart was lying right on top of someone!

Kaleb must already be on the other side of it, because she couldn't see him anywhere. She hurried around it, clearing the way by yelling that she was a doctor. When she reached her destination, she was stunned to see that the victim was an elderly man, his head and torso visible. He was also still conscious, but obviously in agony, moaning, his eyes blankly searching the faces of those gathered around him.

There!

She spied Kaleb kneeling beside the man, along with several other people she recognized from the hospital. His hands were busy feeling beneath the cart. For what? The spot where it was resting on the victim's legs?

How were they going to get it off him? They couldn't just push it back upright. Not without risking crushing the man's legs as the vehicle slid over them a second time.

How, then?

Kaleb conferred with several other people, then stood. "I need about ten men. Four for the front of the vehicle and four for the back. And I need two men to find me some concrete blocks or some heavy timbers."

Volunteers came forward immediately. A police officer arrived as well. Kaleb told him what he needed and the officer got on his radio. Within five minutes there was a pile of concrete blocks.

"We need to lift the golf cart straight up, or

we'll risk injuring him more than he already is. Can I get one person on each end to slide blocks under the cart as we lift it? We'll do it by twos. Push two blocks beneath it, then two more on top of those and so forth, until we can get his legs clear." He glanced around at the assembled group. "Questions?"

Several heads shook.

"Let's get this done, then."

Without a lot of discussion, each man found his spot and waited for the signal. Kaleb had ahold of part of the undercarriage, while Jamie Brooke, the hospital's cardiothoracic surgeon, remained next to the patient's head. "On three. As soon as we lift, you other men shove the first of the blocks beneath the cart."

Maddy joined Jamie, feeling helpless. "We're going to get you out in just a few minutes."

The man didn't respond, but, then again, Maddy hadn't expected him to. Jamie placed two fingers on the side of the victim's neck, taking his pulse as the volunteers got ready to lift.

"...three!"

The golf cart groaned along with several men as they strained to lift the thing. But up it went. Just a few inches, but enough to wedge those bricks underneath it.

The victim cried out for a second, before going quiet again.

Maddy worked with Jamie, trying to see if there was enough room to pull him out, but she couldn't see much space under the vehicle at all. The ground was soft, though, so the first set of blocks had probably sunk a little under the weight of the cart.

The cardiothoracic surgeon called up. "We need to get it higher."

"Right," said Kaleb. "Okay, everyone, on three." A trickle of sweat made its way down his temple, the only visible evidence of the struggle under way. "One…two…*threeeee*."

Up it went another six inches. This time she could see the man's legs. Both of his shins were sliced open from the impact, and there could be crush injuries as well. "I can see his legs." She turned to Jamie. "Can we get him out?"

"I think so."

Kaleb instructed the men to hold their positions while he came around to where Maddy and Jamie were and peered beneath the vehicle. He let out a low curse, probably hoping the same thing everyone else was: that the man hadn't severed any deeper vessels. But they wouldn't know that until they got him free. There was no better person to be on the scene than Jamie, though. He dealt with delicate surgery and blood vessels on a regular basis.

Kaleb looked up at the men who were around the cart. "The blocks should hold the weight, but I need you all to stay there and make sure it doesn't shift as we try to pull him backward."

Kaleb grabbed one of the man's shoulders, while Jamie took hold of the other. They glanced at each other.

"Let's try to make this quick." He nodded at Maddy to clear out of the way. "Okay. Go."

She stood to the side, mentally pulling with the two doctors as they dug in their heels and used the leverage to haul the victim backward with them. Within seconds they had him out from under the cart.

The sound of clapping went up from those around them. Despite the momentary victory, most of those gathered knew that crush injuries could wreak havoc with blood pressure and other vital systems. They weren't out of the woods yet.

She couldn't worry about that now, though. She and Jamie immediately moved to the man's legs to assess his injuries while Kaleb helped the men push the golf cart over until it flipped off the bricks and landed back on its wheels. Twin rust-colored streaks marred the lower edge of the vehicle.

Several more medical professionals gathered around the man, forming their own triage team. Each knew his job and did it well.

Kaleb knelt beside her. "Ambulance is on its way."

"Good."

The man, thank God, had finally passed out from the pain and trauma.

"His legs are intact," Jamie said.

She understood immediately what that meant. Neither limb was severed. His shins were sliced all the way down to the bone and blood oozed in a steady stream down his calves. But somehow, it appeared there were no actual breaks or sliced arteries that she could see. "We need to bind those wounds with something."

A bystander offered up a T-shirt, and Kaleb and Jamie worked to wrap it around both of the man's legs, using a broomstick someone handed them to crank the garment tight enough to compress the wounds without being so tight that it cut off the blood supply completely.

The telltale sound of a siren came from a distance. "Here comes transportation," she said.

Five minutes later, two EMT workers were beside them. Details were relayed to the pair, while Maddy pushed the man's thin white hair off his forehead. He was still out, but he was breathing and his pulse was strong enough. She'd been worried that his blood pressure might bottom out once the cart was lifted off him. It hadn't. He might look frail on the surface, but the man was obviously tough inside. Where it counted.

"Anyone know who he is?" This time it was Kaleb's voice.

Neither of them had even stopped to wonder if he might have relatives nearby. But it was strange that no one had stepped forward.

"I was told he works for the park service." The police officer was back. He checked the man's pockets and found his wallet. "I've got some contact information here." The officer eyed Kaleb and Maddy a little closer. "Don't I know you from somewhere?"

Maddy had no idea what he was talking about. How could he know…?

Oh, Lord. He was the same police officer who'd caught her and Kaleb making out in the park. Heat rushed into her face. Maybe he wouldn't remember them.

Just then the officer's brows went up. "Okay. I've got it." A ghost of a smile played around his lips. "I need to make a few phone calls and see if I can have someone meet him at the hospital.

But I'll need to get a statement from you about what happened."

"We didn't see it happen," Kaleb said. "We just came over to help. We're both doctors. In fact, several of us are."

That seemed to take the officer by surprise. He nodded. "Good thing you were here."

Kaleb checked on their patient again as Jamie and the EMTs got the man ready to transport, passing some last-minute instructions back and forth. They used a backboard to get him onto a stretcher. Once he was on board, the surgeon jumped in with the man and the back doors slammed shut. The driver hopped into the truck, taking off with lights flashing and siren blaring.

"Do you think he's going to be okay?" One of the nurses pushed a strand of dark hair from her face. No one had expected to be called into service today, but no one Maddy could see had walked away without lending a hand.

Kaleb nodded. "He should be, as long as his heart is in good shape."

In the distance, she could see the officer asking people questions and jotting stuff down in a little book. "It's the same officer, you know."

"The same officer?" He gave her a puzzled look.

"The last time we were out here." She swallowed. "He recognized us."

"I still don't follow—" He stopped. "Oh."

"Yeah. Oh. I really hope he's not going to put that in his report anywhere. I would hate for the hospital to get wind of it."

He bumped his shoulder to hers. "It'll be okay."

The same words Kaleb had said about their victim, that he would be okay as long as his heart was in good shape.

It wasn't the *man's* heart she was worried about. It was hers.

And at this point it was a toss-up as to whether or not it was going to be in good shape by the time this was all over with. Or whether it would crash and burn. Just like Roxy's kite.

# CHAPTER SEVEN

THEY WERE ABOUT to announce the winners.

Despite Maddy's warnings about Kaleb not getting too close to her daughter, the little girl had somehow wound up perched on his shoulders. To be able to see the podium, he'd said.

In reality, seeing her up there melted a bigger hole in what was already a sizable chink in her armor. Kaleb held both of Chloe's hands, and her small tennis shoes hit him midchest. Even when her daughter kicked her heels against him in excitement, the muscle mass didn't move. There wasn't an inch of flab beneath that black polo shirt. But there were dusty scuff marks from where her shoes were draped. Maddy's heart clenched. Never once had Matthew held their child like this. And he'd never offered to be involved other than to make threats about taking

Chloe away from her. That had come from a need to hurt her, though. Not from a need to forge a relationship with his daughter.

Yet a man who barely knew them had taken it on himself to help make her happy. First with the kite. And now with this whole day, which Maddy had to admit had been pretty darned magical. A better birthday, she couldn't imagine. Maybe being alone wasn't such a huge treat after all. But she'd already arranged that her sister would take Chloe for the night. So she was stuck with the consequences of her decisions.

Unless that dinner invitation Kaleb had mentioned earlier had been real. So far, he hadn't mentioned it again.

The loudspeaker gave a loud squeal as everyone gathered back in the main assembly area; the kites that had survived the event were back on display alongside their prototypes. Several prizes were due to be awarded, some based on the creativity of design and other aspects. The grand prize, which included the tickets to the Space

Needle and restaurant, was to be awarded to the judges' overall favorite.

"The points from our judges have been tallied, and we'll start with the honorable mention in design and move up from there."

The names and prizes soon became a blur, punctuated by small bursts of applause. Fifteen minutes later neither Roxy's nor Chloe's kite had been named, and Maddy wondered if her daughter was going to be disappointed after all. Well, that was okay. She would have to learn that life didn't always reward hard work. There was often an element of luck involved.

"And now for our grand prize." From Maddy's line of sight, the announcer shuffled pages back and forth, his brow furrowed before evidently finding what he was looking for. A smattering of nervous-sounding laughter swept through the room. "You thought I lost it, didn't you? Yeah, me too. I could just see my spot going to someone else for next year's festival."

He cleared his throat. "Before I announce the winner, though, I want to call Dr. Druthers up to the podium and ask that you all look at the screen to your right."

The crowd's attention shifted to the white area where the monetary goal for the event was listed.

The hospital CEO trotted up the steps to the podium and moved to the microphones, straightening his tie. His eyes went to the blank screen.

"We'd hoped to raise fifty thousand dollars for our pediatric oncology department." He smiled. "Well, folks, thanks to you, we surpassed it. You had those donations pouring in. Our total came to…one hundred and ten thousand, fifty-five dollars and twenty-one cents."

Maddy's eyes widened, especially when the screen flashed the amount along with several pieces of medical equipment that could be purchased with that figure. It was mind-boggling. Maybe it was nothing for Seattle, but for someplace like her hometown that would have been a fortune.

More applause came, this time the sound deafening. Dr. Druthers turned to the screen, adding his applause to the audience's. The announcer waited for it to die down before moving back to the microphone and shaking the CEO's hand. "That is great news for some very special patients."

She glanced toward Kaleb to see if he was smiling as much as she was, but he wasn't. In fact, there was a pale line of pain around his lips that made her wonder if Chloe was getting too heavy for him. Her own smile faded. She touched his arm. He turned toward her, the pain reflected in his eyes as well.

"Do you want me to take her?"

If anything, his expression turned even more haunted, but he shook his head, just as Chloe dug her fingers into his hair as if getting ready to hold on for dear life.

"No." He swallowed. "She's fine, as long as you're okay with it."

"Yes, but…"

Before she could say anything else, the loudspeaker came back to life. "Is everyone ready to hear who our overall winner is?"

"Yes!" The shout went up as one.

"All right, then." The announcer held up his clipboard and peered at it for a minute. "The judges had a hard time picking just one winner, and if it had been based purely on looks and functionality, we might have had a three- or four-way tie. As it was, one entrant added an unusual element to the mix."

Maddy's heart rate picked up, beginning to pump hard in her temples. Surely that had to mean…

"Our winning entry tugged at the judges' heartstrings and so the decision was unanimous." The white-haired gentleman took a dramatic breath. "The prize of four tickets to the Seattle Space Needle goes to Maddy and Chloe Grimes and their high-flying, loud-purring cat, Jetta."

Chloe screamed, leaning down and wrapping her arms around Kaleb's forehead. He seemed to share her happiness, holding her as he turned around in two quick spins. His eyes then met Maddy's. The somber look he'd had moments earlier faded, and he gave her a smile that turned her insides to liquid fire.

"Happy birthday, Maddy." He leaned closer. "If you'll give me your keys, I'll load the stuff in your car in a few minutes. Meet me there after you say goodbye to Chloe and Roxy."

"Okay." She swallowed hard, doing her best not to hear any other motive in his words, and dug in her pocket for her keys, handing them over to him. He'd said nothing else about dinner.

"Come up and get your prize," the announcer said.

*Happy birthday, Maddy.*

Had those low words held a hint of promise? She really hoped so, because that bubble bath was looking less and less like an attractive option, and more like a lonely sentence.

Her sister gave her a quick thumbs-up sign. But when Kaleb acted as if he was going to hand Chloe down to her, she made a quick decision, poking him with her elbow. "Oh, no. You're going up there too. You designed that kite."

Lifting his head, he peered up at her daughter. "What do you think? Do you want me to come with you?"

"Yes!"

Kaleb reached up and wrapped his forearm around Chloe's waist and swept her off his shoulders with a flourish and propped her on his hip. Then they climbed the steps to the podium together. Maddy's only hint of unease about making him accept the prize with them was when they were asked to pose together for a picture for the local paper. But she smiled, hoping no one got any strange ideas about why they were all together. Too late to worry about that now, though.

They were presented with the tickets for the Space Needle and a voucher for dinner reservations at a day and hour of their choosing. Maddy tried to hand them to him, but he shook his head. "You keep them. We'll work out the details later."

More flashes went off indicating pictures being taken. Then they descended the platform. Roxy met her at the bottom and hugged her. "Let me put my stuff in the car. I've got a little something out there for you."

Maddy frowned. "You didn't have to get me anything."

"Are you kidding? Of course I did. You're my baby sister."

Roxy glanced at her watch and then at Kaleb. "Would you mind carrying Chloe out to my car for me? It's later than I expected and I promised Little Miss Kite Winner that I would get us a movie and a pizza to celebrate."

"Sure."

Maddy helped gather the majority of their things, handing Chloe the winning kite—the prototypes for all the kites would go on display in the pediatric oncology ward of the hospital to help cheer its young patients. "Can you carry this for me, honey?"

"Yes." Her daughter cradled the kite carefully against her chest, and Kaleb wound the tail around its body.

Once they had everything loaded in the car and got Chloe strapped into the car seat that Roxy kept in her vehicle, her sister handed her a gift bag out of the back with another hug. "Happy birthday, honey. Enjoy your night. And for what it's worth, I'm really glad you're here in Seattle."

Moisture stung the backs of Maddy's eyelids. She tried to laugh it off before anyone noticed. "You noodle head, there's no place I would rather be."

"Not even home? I know Mom asked you to move back. She told me."

Maddy leaned back and shook her head. "I'm happy at my job, and I love everything about this city. I'm here to stay."

Kaleb did his damnedest not to listen in on their conversation, but he couldn't help but hear the last part of Maddy's statement. She loved everything about this city. He didn't know why, but he was glad that what had happened with her ex wasn't going to drive her back to Nebraska. He realized he had no idea where in Nebraska that was, actually. It was one of a growing list of things he wanted to ask her, however.

Once the sisters had said their goodbyes, Maddy turned to him, her gift bag in hand, the lawn chairs propped against the box that contained her other items. "I know you said you'd put these in the car, but I think I can get it, if you need to get going."

"I'm not in any hurry." He picked up the box and then slung the straps to the chairs' carry bags over his right shoulder. He nodded at Roxy's present. "Don't you want to open that?"

"Oh." She glanced down. "It can wait. Roxy already told me what's inside it. I can get the kite back from Chloe and give it back to you on Monday, if you want to keep it as a memento."

"No. It's hers. I want her to be able to fly it again." He started walking in the direction of her car.

Once everything was tucked into Maddy's vehicle, he leaned against the back bumper. "Let me take you out to dinner. It's your birthday, and I don't feel right sending you back to your apartment by yourself."

"You don't have to do that."

He couldn't tell if she didn't want to go with him or if she was just trying to feel him out. He decided to make it as plain as possible. "You'll find I rarely do anything that I don't want to do."

He touched her cheek. "Go out with me. I want to buy you dinner."

There was a few seconds' pause before she nodded. "Thank you, then. I'd like that. It's been a busy day, but I was actually kind of regretting promising Chloe she could go home with Roxy. I'd need to run home and check on Jetta and feed him first, though, if you don't mind."

"It's on our way. We can drop off your car in the process, if that's okay?"

"More than okay."

When he followed her up to the elevator of her apartment building, his arms full, they found a box sitting in front of her door. And from the imprinted logo on the side along with the scent of ginger that lingered in the hallway, someone had already made dinner plans for Maddy. So much for taking her out. Maybe it was just as well. Because standing in her hallway reminded him of Maddy's original plan of soaking in the tub.

She opened the door, pushing the box inside with her foot. Jetta met them almost immediately, meowing and winding around her in a way that made him smile. That was a lot of effort to garner sympathy. The cat had been working on that act for a while, from the looks of it.

"I take it he's hungry."

She laughed. "He's always hungry." Motioning to the stuff he was holding, she said, "You can just set that anywhere, and if you don't mind putting the take-out box on the counter, I'd appreciate it. I'll rustle up some food for Jetta. He's earned it for inspiring the kite design. I guess this means we don't have to go out for dinner after all."

Hearing her say the words punched his gut in a way he didn't like. Hadn't he just been thinking that himself?

"I guess not. I'll leave you to your meal, then."

She turned around in a flash. "What? You're going?"

"I assumed…" He nodded at the box. "I'm sure that's a meal for one."

"If I know Roxy, it's enough for five or ten people." She glanced down for a moment at the cat, who was still meowing up a storm, before looking back at him. "Please stay, Kaleb. I thought I wanted to be alone, but…"

"Are you sure?"

"Yes, I really am. And if there isn't enough in that box—although I know there will be—we can call out for more to supplement it."

Kaleb set the items he'd brought in next to a floral padded bench she had just inside her door. Then he picked up the box of food and set it on the counter as she'd asked him to do. "Where are your plates?" He peered into the box and saw several cardboard containers inside. There was indeed quite an assortment of food, from the looks of it.

"In the cabinet to the left of the sink."

While she popped the top on a can of cat food and scooped the contents into a small silver bowl inside a walk-in pantry, he found plates, silverware and glasses and set the dining-room table.

By the time she came back in the room, he had the cartons unloaded from the box and the plates set on bamboo place mats. There were a couple of candles poking from a centerpiece, but he didn't want to light them and risk her thinking he was pushing for things that he wasn't.

Was he sure about that?

"Wow, thanks. I didn't expect you to do all of that."

She put the gift bag on the far end of the table.

"I didn't know it was your birthday before today, or I would have gotten you something."

"Why?"

Kaleb hadn't expected the bald question, so he shifted for a second, trying to figure out a good answer for what had been an impulsive statement. "Because you work hard, and you deserve it. Just like Roxy thinks you do. You have a good sister, you know."

"Oh, I know. She rescued me." As if realizing that sounded a little weird, she continued. "Matthew was getting harder and harder to avoid in my little hometown. Gamble Point, Nebraska, actually. Roxy suggested I move to the city and make a clean break of it. I never expected him to follow me. If he'd hurt anyone, I never would have—"

"He didn't, Maddy."

"I know, but…" She shook her head as if trying to blot out that horrific image. "Anyway, sit down. And thanks for staying."

"Thanks for asking me."

Just then her cell phone rang. He nodded toward her purse. "Feel free."

"I'll just be a minute." She got out her phone and glanced at the readout. "It's my mom. I'll try to make it quick."

"Take your time."

While Maddy talked to her mother, who had obviously called to wish her a happy birthday, Kaleb wandered around the living room, glancing at pictures of her and various family members on the mantelpiece. One of the shots was of a woman with the same curly hair as Maddy, threaded with a few strands of gray. That had to be her mother.

He peered closer. He could certainly see where Maddy and Roxy got their looks. A man in bib overalls had to be her father. She'd mentioned that he died in a tractor accident and the snapshot was older than the one of her mom. He didn't see any other ones of the man. A twinge of pain cramped his lungs for a moment. His own parents were still very much alive. Still very much hoping for another grandchild, although Kaleb didn't see that happening anytime soon, if ever. The genetic dice hadn't rolled in his favor the first time, and he couldn't guarantee the outcome would be any better a second time. He couldn't see himself putting his heart—or a child's life—at risk like that. Once had been more than enough.

Having Chloe propped on his shoulders had re-awakened feelings that were better off left dead. And Maddy obviously felt the same way about Chloe getting attached to another man.

He picked up a picture of Maddy holding a bundle wrapped in a hospital blanket. She was smiling, but the curve of her lips seemed uncertain and more than a little sad. He studied the picture. Her hair was longer than it was now, but she still had the same expressive eyes. The same high cheekbones. The woman from the previous picture was also present, leaning down beside Maddy, her cheek pressed to her daughter's. Matthew was not in the picture, although it was possible she had got rid of any reminders of what must have been a terribly unhappy and unstable marriage. He set the picture back down, a rumble starting up in his gut that wasn't caused by hunger.

Something had happened, even back then. But it wasn't his place to ask. Especially since the last thing he wanted to do was exchange confidences about their pasts. He didn't want to talk about Grace. Or his own failed marriage. At least Maddy still had her child.

"Sorry about that. She wanted to wish me a happy birthday."

He nodded at the picture he'd just held. "Is that her?"

Maddy glanced at it. "Yes. I'm trying to talk her into moving to Seattle, but she doesn't want to leave Nebraska."

"You have her eyes. Her smile."

"Thank you. I love my mother's smile. She's a truly kind woman."

"I can believe that, judging from the pictures. But then again, so are you."

Something in the atmosphere changed slightly as Maddy's eyes met his. "D-do you want to eat?"

Eat. Yes. That was the thing he should do.

Instead, he moved a step or two closer. "Happy birthday, again, Maddy. Has it been a good one?"

"It has. Especially now."

He wasn't sure exactly how it happened, but he cupped her face, meaning to give her a quick birthday kiss. But when his lips touched hers, they suddenly had a mind of their own and lingered a little longer than he'd meant them to. When Maddy didn't move to break the contact, he slid an arm behind her back and edged her another step closer. Still no protest on her part.

To hell with it. They were both grown-ups. If they spent a night together, it was no big deal. She'd said herself she didn't want to spend her birthday alone. Well, he didn't want to spend the night alone either, and it had been forever since he'd been with anyone. She'd made it clear that she wanted no ties to a man. And he wanted no commitments to a woman.

It was the perfect marriage.

No. Not marriage. It was the perfect arrangement. An arrangement that would last a single night. Maybe not even that long.

*But you're in her house. Off your own turf.*

It didn't matter, because there was no question about where Maddy's loyalties lay. With her daughter and no one else. He just needed to be certain they were on the same page. He eased back. Landed a few more kisses on her soft lips. "How hungry are you?"

Her hands went to the back of his neck. "Pretty hungry."

His gut sank before coming back up. The way she'd said that… "Hungry. For dinner?"

"Do you need to ask?"

No, he didn't, since she was holding on to him as tightly as he was holding her. This time when he kissed her, he did it without holding back, landing his mouth on hers and slanting over it. His fingers went underneath her tank top, finding the warm skin of her waist before sliding around to her bare back. She was impossibly silky and smooth, and he couldn't stop one of his hands from running up her spine, feeling the bumps of her vertebrae beneath his seeking fingertips.

Wanting to touch more of her, he found the hem of her shirt and tugged it up, unlocking their lips long enough to haul it over her head before finding her mouth again. This time, his tongue slid in to find hers.

The woman tasted like mint with an edge of sweetness that was all Maddy. And he couldn't get enough of her.

Her hands went to his chest, splaying over it as he pulled her closer. He found her bra clasp and the need to unhook it thrummed within him. But he wanted to enjoy this. Every second of it.

He hadn't planned on coming back to her place and doing this, but, now that it had happened, he was going to make it last. If this was going to be the only time he had with her, he wasn't going to punt a field goal when he could run the play all the way home.

Pulling free from her for a couple more seconds, he yanked his own shirt over his head, taking a moment to look at her. Clad in a lacy black bra, casual capri pants and her sandals, the woman was gorgeous. Her lips were pink from his kisses, her hair in glorious disarray from the breeze earlier. She looked like a modern-day Eve. A temptress who was holding out a very different kind of fruit. One he couldn't wait to taste. To savor. Until he'd devoured every last bite.

"I'm glad I had Roxy take Chloe after all."

"Are you?" He leaned in and nipped her bottom lip. "What about that bubble bath you were looking forward to?"

"I'm still looking forward to it."

He frowned. Maybe he'd misunderstood her. But no. They were both standing there partially clothed.

Maddy hooked a finger in the waistband of his jeans. "The present Roxy gave me—it's everything I need for a relaxing night in the tub. Bath salts, bubbles. A loofah."

"A what?"

"It's a… You'll have to experience it to understand. But it's heavenly."

It couldn't be any more heavenly than what he was looking at right now. "And you're telling me this because?"

"Because the bathtub in this apartment is oversized."

His body went on high alert. "Are you saying it's more than enough for one person?"

"I'm saying it's more than enough for two people. That tub was what sold me on the apartment. It seemed like the perfect place to unwind after a hard day." She grinned. "Except, I think I've only gotten to use it once."

"I'm sure it's hard when you have a child pounding down the door."

"Exactly. But there's no child right now. And Jetta isn't overly fond of water. So I'm pretty sure we're safe."

"*Safe* is a relative word." One side of his mouth went up. "Are you inviting me into your tub, Dr. Grimes?"

"It depends on whether or not you'd accept the offer."

"I don't think there's any question of that. It's more of a question of how long it will take to fill that tub."

"How about if I go in and get it started and then call you when I'm ready?"

Maddy scooted beneath a mountain of bubbles until only her head and neck were showing. The second thoughts that had churned to life the second she'd turned on the tap had now morphed into third and fourth thoughts. It was probably too late to back out now, though, especially since she was completely naked and was pretty sure Kaleb was waiting on the other side of that door. She could always send him away. But she didn't want to.

So what was the problem?

The problem was she hadn't done this in a very long time. And the last time had been when she was pregnant with Chloe, and it had been terrible. Matthew had barely been able to look at her back then. And now she had stretch marks and a little more meat on her hips than she'd had in her younger years. What if she saw the same look of disgust in Kaleb's eyes that she'd witnessed in Matthew's?

She should tell him to leave. Now. Before he had a chance to see her.

No. She was buried beneath the bubbles. It was one of the reasons she'd told him about Roxy's gifts. It gave her an excuse to whip the water into a frothy mass that covered everything. He could feel her, and they could make love, but it wouldn't be like lying naked on the bed, her every flaw exposed to his eyes.

Yes. She wanted to do this. Despite her fears, she had a feeling that Kaleb, despite all the flirting he did, would be a passionate but fair lover. He wouldn't expect perfection. At least she hoped he wouldn't.

She sank even lower, mounding more bubbles over her breasts.

"Everything okay in there?"

She'd turned the water off minutes ago, so he

must be wondering what was taking so long. "Yes."

"Well, may I come in?" There was a thread of amusement in his voice.

"Do you promise not to laugh?"

This time there was a prolonged pause. "Why would I laugh?"

Her face flamed to life. Did he want her to spell it out? "Because I'm not…I'm not…I don't want you to laugh at me."

"Maddy, the last thing I feel like doing right now is laughing." The doorknob turned, but he didn't shove the door open immediately. "I'm coming in. If you don't want me to, you'd better tell me now."

She bit her tongue to keep herself from shouting for him to stay out.

The door opened just enough for him to slide through. Maddy half expected him to burst into the room fully naked, ready for action. But the man was dressed exactly as she'd left him. His chest was bare, but he still had on his jeans, which were slung low around his lean hips. Even his shoes and socks were still in place.

He closed the door and leaned against it, studying her for several heart-pounding seconds. Long enough that she wondered if the bubbles had dissipated, allowing him to see her through the water. She forced herself to keep meeting his eyes, refusing to cower, even though she wanted nothing more than to leap from the tub, grab the nearest towel and cocoon herself in it.

Moving from his post, he sat on the very edge of the tub. "Why would I laugh?"

She swallowed. "I've had a child. My body isn't… It isn't like it used to be."

"You're beautiful. I don't need to see you naked to know that." He dipped a finger beneath the bubbles and scooped up a small amount, plopping it onto her nose. He smiled. "Still not laughing."

"Thank you." The simple words almost got stuck in her throat but she forced them out.

He leaned down and kissed her mouth. "Are you sure there's room in there for me?"

"Oh, yes."

With that, he stood up and toed off one shoe and then the other while she watched. He rolled off his socks, revealing strong feet, the slightest dusting of dark hair across the top giving them a decidedly masculine edge. Maddy's mouth watered.

He was going to be in the tub in a few more seconds and those hands would touch her all over. Only this time there would be no clothes between them.

His wallet came out of his pocket. He opened it. Took out a condom from a little side section. Lord, she hoped that was something he always carried and not something he'd put in there just for this occasion.

Maybe he saw the uncertainty on her face because he stopped and traced a line down the length of her jaw. "I wasn't scheming to get into your bed when I left my house this morning, if that's what you're wondering."

"Of course not." But it was, and they both knew it.

Some woman was going to be very lucky to

have him one day. For a second she wished it were her, before shutting down that line of thought completely. She had Chloe to think about. And there was no way she was going to set up her daughter to be hurt by a man. She hadn't allowed Matthew to do that. And she wasn't going to risk it with anyone else. Not right now. Maybe when Chloe was old enough to understand that relationships were never a certainty.

She shook that from her thoughts before she ruined everything.

Kaleb fished his keys from one of his front pockets and set them on the side of the sink. Then he smiled. "Do you have a dryer?"

"Yes, of course, but why do you—"

She hadn't even got the words out of her mouth before Kaleb stepped into the bathtub, still clad in his jeans.

"What are you doing?" The words came out as a choked laugh.

"Showing you that there's nothing wrong with a little laughter." He grinned and slid his body into the water until he was facing her, the bottoms of his feet sliding up her calves, over her knees and working their way up her thighs. "As long as that laughter ends with me making love to you."

## CHAPTER EIGHT

HIS JEANS WERE staying on. Because if he took them off, it was all over. The look of shock on her face had made the pain of not being able to immediately take what he wanted a little easier to bear. He would get there. Soon enough.

"So this is your tub." He stretched both arms along the ledge on either side of him. Set into the corner of the room, the white fixture was definitely big enough for the both of them. He was able to fully extend his legs without a problem. The only thing wrong with the setup was that she'd put so many damned bubbles into the water, he couldn't see a thing.

*Do you promise not to laugh?*

When he'd realized what she meant, the words had hit his gut like a freight train. He couldn't imagine anyone laughing at Maddy.

But she'd felt insecure enough to think that he might.

"Was I right about its size?"

"You were. It's far too big for my liking, in fact."

Her eyes widened in surprise. "It is?"

"Absolutely. You are much too far away." With that, he ducked his arms beneath the water until he found her calves. He wrapped his fingers around them and tugged. Maddy came sliding toward him with a small screech. She laughed again, making him smile. "That's better."

He slid his ankles around her backside, his body erupting with need when his bare feet met nothing but her skin. Okay, so the jeans might not have been a good idea after all. He was going to have a hell of a time getting them off when the time came. Especially since he could well imagine which parts of her body were now resting against his lower half.

Trying to forget about that, he cupped her face and leaned in to kiss her, taking up where they'd left off in the other room. Maddy's hands went to his shoulders, her wet fingers warm from being submerged in the water.

"You need to take your jeans off."

The whispered words echoed his earlier thoughts.

"I will in a few minutes." Some kind of long beige sponge lay to the left of them along the edge of the tub. He touched it, surprised to find it wasn't soft and spongy at all, but firm.

"That's the loofah." She took it from him and poured some kind of liquid onto it. "Turn around."

"Not a chance." The last thing he wanted to do was face away from her.

She leaned in and kissed his cheek, her chin rubbing along his jawline. "I promise I'll make it worth your while."

Dammit. Now she had him thinking all kinds of crazy things. Unhooking his ankles from behind her, he stood, turning to face the far wall, which had a large mirror attached. He sank back into the water, his eyes meeting Maddy's. This time, she was the one with the smile.

"Back up so I can reach you."

He did just that, her legs coming around his, feet tucking beneath his thighs. The sponge connected with his back and she scrubbed with just enough pressure to make his nerve endings stand up and sing. "Hell."

Maddy laughed. "Really? Because I always thought it felt like heaven."

Heaven. Hell. They were kind of all squashed together in his head right now.

Leaning forward a bit, he closed his eyes, unable to keep a low groan from coming out. She continued to move the sponge over him, gradually working her way up until she reached his shoulders.

Then something soft pressed against the skin of his back and his eyes popped open just as he realized what it was. Her breasts. Before he could do anything, Maddy looped her arms over his shoulders, sliding the top of the sponge down his chest and over his abdomen until it dipped beneath the water. Then it pressed against a part of him that was beginning to protest. Loudly. Insistently.

He grabbed the sponge from her and set it back where it came from.

"Now, Maddy," he said, staring at her in the mirror and realizing he was fighting a battle he had no desire to win. "Now it's time to lose the jeans."

Something was tickling her ear.

Not physically, but…

Sound. The gentle trill of…an alarm clock?

No. She shifted her hand and met warm flesh. She snuggled closer, an arm coming around her waist and dragging her fully against him.

And there were no jeans to come between them this time.

The noise came again. Melodic. Distant.

A phone? She blinked her eyes open for a second. Her hand slid along his bare arm, enjoying the rough feel of masculine hair against her palm.

The singsong tune morphed into something not so pleasant. She didn't want to listen to it anymore. In fact, she didn't want to listen to anything except…

Something banged repeatedly against a hard surface.

The figure behind her sat up and turned her onto her back, a slight smile playing around the edges of his mouth.

Kaleb. Wow. So it hadn't been a dream.

None of it. Heat swept over her body as she remembered the second he'd lowered that zipper.

Light peeked around the edges of her curtains. It was morning.

Something pounded again. It was a little too early for repairs, wasn't it?

"Someone's at your door." His thumb came out to slide along her lower lip. A shiver went over her.

She stretched, enjoying what met her eyes. His chest was naked, the sheet just barely covering his…

…*at the door?*

"Maddy? Hello? Are you home?"

A voice… The sound was no longer outside, but inside the apartment!

*Inside!*

Wrenching herself upright, she stared at Kaleb, no longer in admiration, but in abject panic as she recognized the sound. "It's my sister," she hissed. "You have to get out of here. Now!"

He leaned closer, that lazy grin sliding across his face. "Do you want me to leap from your window?"

"No, I just…" She cleared her throat and made her voice loud enough to be heard. "Just a second, Roxy. I'm just now getting up."

Scrambling from the bed, she stripped his shirt from her chest and tossed it at him. "You. Dressed. Now!"

Maddy dragged her clothes on as fast as humanly possible, not caring that it was the same outfit she'd worn yesterday. Then she yanked her fingers through her tangled hair. "Coming."

She didn't stop to check whether or not Kaleb was doing what she asked; she simply whisked through the bedroom door, pulling it shut behind her. As long as she could keep Roxy—or worse, Chloe—from discovering that Kaleb

McBride had spent the night in her bed, she would be fine. She hoped.

The man had to have known he rocked her world. No one had made love to her like that in... well, forever. There were no comparisons, and that scared the hell out of her.

She strolled down the hall and into the living room, wearing the biggest smile she could muster. "Hey, you two..."

Her voice died. Because, yes, Roxy and Chloe were there. In fact, her daughter launched herself into her arms and hung on tight. But standing just behind them was someone she hadn't expected.

"Mom? What are you doing here?"

Keeping one arm around Chloe, she glanced back at the bedroom, hoping against hope that Kaleb was not going to pull that door open and let everyone know he was there.

Roxy, she could handle; her sister had had her share of lovers over the years. Not so much recently, but in their younger days. Maddy could have even come up with some kind of funny explanation for Kaleb being here—although nothing sounded particularly humorous to her at the moment.

But her mom?

Oh, no. She would see right through the ploy. She would know. She always did.

Her mom laughed and came over to kiss her cheek. "I'm happy to see you too, dear." She glanced around the room. "You've been trying to get me to come out here for a visit for a while, and after…well, what happened with Matthew, I wanted to see where you lived. I would have come for your birthday yesterday, but Roxy told me she'd promised you a night alone."

Oh, Lord. She'd definitely not been alone. Not then. And not now.

"Mommy? My head hurts."

The words came from Chloe, and while she did her best to concentrate on what they meant, she was still trying to figure out why her mom had really come. Today of all days. How was she going to get Kaleb out of that room?

"I'm sorry, sweetheart," Maddy said. "Do you need some medicine?"

"No. It's not a sicky headache, just a normal one." Chloe got migraines from time to time, but it had been months since her last one. She always wondered if she'd handed her daughter some kind of defective gene. If maybe her asthma had passed itself off as migraines in Chloe. Ridiculous. She knew it was, but there was always a tiny shard of guilt every time her daughter suffered through one of her bad headaches.

She decided she was going to have to enlist her sister's help if she was going to get through this. "Chloe, how about if you show Nana your room? Jetta was sleeping on your bed last time I saw him. Maybe he's still there."

So what if the last time she'd seen the cat was after midnight, just as Kaleb was carrying her to bed after making love to her in the bathroom? Maybe the cat really was still there.

"Sure! C'mon, Nana. It's right down this hallway."

Her mom threw Maddy a quick frown, but followed her granddaughter. As soon as they were out of earshot, she grabbed Roxy's arm. "You've got to keep them in there for about five minutes."

Her sister tilted her head. "What are you talking about?"

"There's no time to explain." She half dragged her down the hallway. "Just do it. Please."

Maddy stopped with her hand on the doorknob to her bedroom. Her sister's eyes got wide. She whispered, "You...you've got a *man* in there."

That struck her as insanely funny for some reason. "Well, it's certainly not a pony."

"Oh, my God, Maddy. You are so going to spill when this is all over."

At this point, she didn't care what she had to do. So long as Kaleb was on his way out of her apartment before her mother came out of that room.

Roxy hurried down the hallway, her voice much louder than necessary. "I haven't seen good old Jetta in ages. Can I join in?" Her sister threw Maddy one last grin before disappearing into the room.

Before she could turn the knob on her own

bedroom door, it opened so fast she practically fell inside.

"You have to leave," she whispered. "Right now."

"That's what I'm trying to do." His voice didn't sound nearly as friendly as it had a few minutes ago. "What's wrong with Chloe?"

"Wrong?" She tried to hurry him along, thanking God they'd had the foresight to throw his jeans into the dryer last night. She did her best not to remember how those same jeans had felt scraping over her legs as he'd climbed into the tub.

"She said her head hurt."

"Oh. Yes. She gets headaches periodically. She's fine."

Kaleb's face unexpectedly blanched, turning a sickly white. Probably worried about getting caught, just as she was. She wouldn't be surprised if her own face was rather pasty right now.

They made it to the front door, and she quietly opened it. "Thanks for everything." She closed her eyes for a minute. "I mean… Well, you know what I mean."

"Yes." He stepped outside the door and paused. "Have you had them looked at?"

"Sorry?" She was doing her best to keep her voice down to a whisper, but she was running out of time. And patience.

"The headaches."

"We've already been to a couple of specialists." She did her best to smile. "I really, really don't want my mom to find you here. Sorry." With that, she shut the door with as soft a click as she could and prayed he hadn't left anything lying…

Yanking in a quick breath, she raced through the hallway and glanced into the bathroom. Nothing there, thank God. She tiptoed back a few steps to peek into her room. Unmade bed, but that was to be expected. It was barely—she glanced at her watch—eight o'clock.

Just then she spotted two towels beside the bed. She went in and grabbed them, hoping she could hurry to the bathroom and throw them over a towel bar. Just as she came out of the room, her mom and the rest of her entourage appeared. And two pairs of adult eyes swung to her hands, which clutched one blue towel and one white towel. Her mom's eyes slowly shifted back to hers, a question in them Maddy had no intention of answering.

"Just cleaning up from last night." Realizing how that sounded, she hurried to add, "Roxy kept Chloe for me and sent me home with a bag of spa treatment goodies, and so I took full advantage of it."

"Full advantage. I'll say." Roxy's amused voice held a wealth of meaning, but Maddy ignored it the best she could.

"One towel for my hair and one for the rest of me."

Her mom's brows cranked up in steady increments. "Why are you explaining, dear?"

"Well, because…" She was so going to get struck by lightning for lying. "…I wouldn't want you to get any strange ideas."

"I'll just put these away so you can go make us some coffee. It looks like you could use some."

Roxy plucked the towels from her hand, leaning down to whisper, "If she didn't have any ideas before, she certainly does now."

"Just what I need," Maddy breathed in return. But really she was glad to have something to do. And that Kaleb had made it out of the house unnoticed.

Just then the doorbell rang. Oh, no! What more could possibly happen? She looked through the peephole and was met by a familiar face. Her heart careened through her chest. Sending up a quick prayer, she opened the door and pretended he was a complete stranger. "Yes? Can I help you?"

Kaleb wasn't smiling. And the flirtatious demeanor from this morning was long gone. But at least he kept his voice low. "I think I left my keys in your bathroom."

Roxy appeared beside her. She glanced at Maddy and then at the man in the entryway. "I think you might be looking for these." She let the keys dangle from her fingertips.

"Yes, that's them. Thank you." He took them from her with a perfunctory smile.

Then the worst thing that could have happened did. Without a word to her, Maddy's mother marched right up to him and held out her hand.

"Since my daughters have evidently forgotten all their manners, hello, my name is Linda."

A muscle worked in his jaw, but he shook her hand. "I'm Kaleb McBride. I work at the hospital where your daughter practices."

Her mom blinked. "Nice to meet you. You work there as a…"

"I practice concierge medicine." As if anticipating her next question, he added, "The hospital has a contract with the hotel across the street. I split my time between the two places."

She could practically see the wheels in her mom's head turning, rotating far too many times for comfort. Two towels. A colleague leaving his keys at her place. Her granddaughter staying with Roxy overnight.

*Please don't.*

She sent her mother a quick look begging her

not to take this line of questioning any further. Instead her mom nodded. "Well, it was nice to meet someone that Maddy works with." She took her granddaughter's hand. "Now, if you'll tell me where that medicine is for her headache, I'll get it for her."

"It's already all better," Chloe said. "It wasn't one of the mean ones."

Her mom leaned down to kiss Chloe's cheek. "I'm glad."

"Could I have a glass of apple juice, though?"

Maddy swallowed, glad for the distraction and an excuse to send them away for a few more minutes. "Chloe, would you show Nana where the glasses and juice are? And see if she wants something to drink as well."

"I'll show them."

Roxy was being extraordinarily helpful all of a sudden, moving away with the duo and talking a mile a minute about the kite festival.

Once again, she was left alone with Kaleb.

He flipped his keys into his palm, brown eyes meeting hers. "Sorry about that. I got all the way to my car and realized I forgot to put them back in my pocket."

She'd forgotten as well. But now she could see it happen all over again in her mind's eye. Kaleb's big hand sliding into the front pocket of his jeans as he slowly extracted his keys and dropped them on the vanity in the bathroom. Of the way her breath hitched in her throat when she realized he was going to step into her tub without removing his pants. She wasn't likely to forget what they'd done. Not for a long, long time.

It was then and there that Maddy realized she was in serious trouble. She'd dug herself a deep pit and had hopped right into it, not thinking about the consequences of her actions. And now she was stuck at the bottom with no way to escape. But she'd better either figure it out or find a ladder tall enough to climb to the top. And soon. Because if she didn't, her mom would discover what she'd done last night. And not only her mother. But her sister, her daughter and probably the whole damn hospital.

# CHAPTER NINE

"I DON'T WANT to go to the hospital."

The woman lying in the bed in her hotel room was in obvious respiratory distress, her words coming out in a disjointed series of wheezes that reminded him of his encounter with Maddy in the lobby of this very hotel.

Last week had thrown him for a loop, and he realized what a huge mistake he had made by staying at her place. It was why he never stayed at a woman's house. The less he knew, the easier it was to walk away when the night was over.

Instead, he'd wandered around Maddy's living room, looking at intimate glimpses of her life. He'd even met her mother, for goodness' sake. Something that never would have happened if he'd stuck to his internal rule book. He could have brought her back to his own place and made love to her without a care in the world. But no. He had to go and act as if he could do whatever he wanted without it costing one red cent.

How wrong he'd been.

Chloe saying that her head hurt had sent a shaft of pain through him that had cut him to the core. He'd heard that same phrase almost word for word from his own daughter. "Daddy, my head hurts."

A few weeks later, she'd been diagnosed with an inoperable brain tumor.

Forcing his attention back to his patient, he put the stethoscope in his ears and asked her to sit up for a minute. "When I tell you to, can you breathe deeply for me?"

"I'll try."

He pressed the chest piece of the instrument to her back. "Okay, breathe."

Where Kaleb should have heard deep clear chest sounds, there was an ominous crackling instead, that originated in the lower lobe of Gloria Lowell's right lung. He moved it a little higher. "Again."

The crackling sound diminished dramatically the higher he got. He moved to the other side and had his patient take another deep breath. There it was again. Bi-basal crackling. Could be pneumonia. Could be something interstitial. But whatever it was, it wasn't going away without treatment.

Her husband, who was standing nearby, must have seen something in his face. "What is it?"

"She needs to go to the hospital." It was his second attempt to convince Gloria to head across the street. He addressed her directly. "I need to do a chest X-ray. You could have pneumonia."

"Are you sure?" She gave a labored cough that left her gasping for breath all over again.

"That you have pneumonia? No. But I am hearing some sounds in your lungs that are cause for concern. Your husband can stay with you every step of the way."

Mrs. Lowell had to be pushing seventy-five or maybe eighty. Lung infections at that age were worrisome. The couple was in Seattle on a whirlwind vacation. He could understand why she didn't want to wind up in a hospital so far away from home.

As his daughter had?

They too had been on vacation when Grace had got her first headache. They'd gone to an emergency room, and had left with antibiotics. But things had got better, so they chalked it up to a sinus infection. In the end, they'd waited until they got home to follow up with their regular doctor, not knowing it was already too late. If he'd just taken her symptoms more seriously, would things have ended differently?

"It's right across the street. We won't even need to call an ambulance." He crossed his fingers mentally, hoping this would work and that Gloria wouldn't board her scheduled flight later on today. "I have a friend who can bring a wheelchair over from the hospital. We'll just take you across, and if nothing's wrong we'll bring you right back. You still have several hours before you need to be at the airport."

He prayed what he was thinking would work. "Clyde? You'll stay with me?"

He took ahold of her hand. "Always, baby."

The obvious love between the husband and wife made his gut tighten. If Grace had lived, would he and Janice have made it until "death do us part"? Although if their relationship had been strong enough, it should have survived even Grace's illness and death. But it hadn't.

Gloria took a deep breath and then immediately went into another coughing fit. Once she stopped, she nodded. "Okay. But no ambulances. My daddy died after going to the hospital in one of those."

"No ambulance." He paused. "Let me just make a quick call."

Pulling out his cell phone, he hoped he wasn't making a terrible mistake. It had been less than a week since he'd spent the night with Maddy. She could very well hang up on him. He knew he'd acted like a jerk on his way out of her house, but Chloe's headache…

Damn.

He pressed the numbers for the hospital and then asked the operator to connect him with

Maddy. He waited as the line started ringing. He could only hope she wasn't with a patient and picked up rather than letting the phone go straight to voice mail. Although once she realized who it was, she might very well not answer it.

The ringer sounded for the third time when he heard a familiar click. "Dr. Grimes."

"Maddy? It's Kaleb."

"Hi."

"Sorry to bother you, but I have a patient over here at the Consortium. Breathing problems—"

"Asthma?" The tone of her voice immediately shifted, moving into the realm of a professional in a single breath.

"Bilateral crackles."

"Can you bring the patient in?"

He hesitated, then forged ahead. "She doesn't want an ambulance. I told her that I would try to arrange a wheelchair transport."

"A wheelchair what?"

"Are you busy with patients right now?"

"Not right this second. Do you want me to come over and take a look?"

Well, at least she didn't sound irritated. "Would you? It's the only way I can get her to agree to get checked out."

"I'll be right there." She paused. "And I'll bring that wheelchair with me, just in case."

Maddy arrived at the hotel ten minutes later. When she went into the lobby, the concierge was expecting her. He came right over. "She's on the tenth floor, room 1021. Do you want me to go up with you?"

"No, I'll be fine."

Would she? She no longer knew.

She walked over to the bank of elevators, pushing the wheelchair. It only took a minute until she was headed up to the patient's floor. She had no idea how she was going to feel when she saw Kaleb's face. She'd been actively trying to avoid him ever since he'd left her place. Her mom coming to spend the week with her had not only put a crimp in her schedule, but it had also brought a lot of other complications. She'd begun hinting that it was time for Maddy to start looking for love again. Reminders that Matthew had died a little less than a month ago had done nothing to deter her. And Maddy's attempts to get her mom to change her mind about moving to Seattle had also fallen on deaf ears.

Did she really want her mom here, messing in her business?

She closed her eyes. Since when did she consider it messing?

Since Kaleb?

*Ping!*

The sound came just as she was mulling over the answer to that question.

She shook her head and pushed the wheelchair out of the elevator. And the man she'd been worried about seeing was in the hallway, waiting for her. The air left her lungs in a rush.

It was bad. Just as bad as she expected. Her legs trembled and her mouth went completely dry in the space of a few seconds.

The man did it for her. Really, really did it, in a way that no man ever had, and that included Matthew.

She swallowed and forced as normal a smile as she could, even though her heart was beating out of her chest. "You called for a chariot?"

"I did indeed." He gave her a smile in return that was a lot warmer than hers had been. "Thank you. I owe you."

"No, you don't. Tell me what's going on."

Within two minutes he'd filled her in on the situation. He then introduced her to Gloria and her husband. Kaleb hadn't been exaggerating. The patient's breathing sounded labored and there was a definite congested rattle to it. They needed to get her to the hospital. The woman was in no hurry to leave, though, despite how hard it was for her to catch her breath.

Maddy sat on the bed next to her. "Tell me why you're afraid to go."

Gloria's eyes tracked away to her husband and then back. "My father went to the hospital. He never came out."

That she could understand. When she glanced up at Kaleb, he was standing by the big bank of windows looking out over the city.

"What happened?" she asked.

"He had a heart attack. I was just a girl. They wouldn't let me go into the room." Her chin wobbled a time or two and she took a gasping breath that was half cry, half cough. "I never saw him again."

Maddy's heart ached for the little girl Gloria had once been.

"Are you worried that will happen to you?"

"Dr. McBride said that Clyde could stay with me. Is that true?"

She glanced again at the window, and this time, Kaleb had turned to stare at her. Was he wondering if she was going to contradict him? She would have promised Gloria the very same thing had she been in his position.

"Yes, you'll be in my department, so I can let the nurses know. He doesn't have to leave your side except when they take X-rays, but he'll be right around the corner behind the screen with the technician. Will that be okay?"

Her husband laid his hand on her shoulder. "Tell them you'll go, Gloria."

"Yes," she whispered. "I'll go."

Within a matter of minutes, they had her loaded up in the wheelchair and Kaleb was pushing her out of the hotel toward the crosswalk. It could have been any family out for a stroll, but it wasn't. And it was dangerous for Maddy to even allow herself to think along those lines. She had Chloe to think about. Just like Gloria, who had never been able to see her father, her daughter had never seen a *real* father. Matthew had not wanted to be a father. He'd been an unwilling sperm donor at best. At worst he'd been willing to kill his daughter's mother, and possibly even Chloe. Who knew what he would have done had he got into her office? Would he have gone to Roxy's and killed her too, before turning that gun on her daughter and then himself?

*Kaleb is nothing like Matthew.*

No, but, as good as he'd been with Chloe, there had definitely been moments when he'd seemed uncomfortable around her. As if he couldn't wait to get away from her.

Thankfully she was soon in the hospital, where

she could concentrate on the task at hand: seeing what was going on with Gloria's breathing. They'd barely got up to the radiology department, though, when Gloria gasped harder, her breathing suddenly going haywire before she slumped over in the wheelchair.

"She's in respiratory failure. We need to get her flat." Kaleb was beside them in an instant, lifting the frail woman out of the wheelchair and bodily carrying her to the nearest curtained-off area, laying her on the bed. Maddy yelled for help and several nurses immediately stepped into the cubicle, going to work to get her stable. Her husband was in the room with her, and Maddy didn't have the heart to ask him to step out. Not yet. She'd promised Gloria that he could stay, and she didn't want to go back on that if she didn't have to.

"Do you want to intubate her?"

"Let's try NPPV, before we do that. She wasn't febrile?"

"She was, but she took ibuprofen, so her temperature is artificially lowered at this point."

Maddy nodded, her brain taking in that bit of information. "I still want to get an X-ray, but we'll have to do it in the supine position."

They fastened the breathing mask over Gloria's face, hoping the positive pressure ventilator would help avoid standard intubation. Within a minute, her color looked a little better. "Let's get her into X-ray and see what's going on."

Once they were in the room, they rolled Gloria to the side in order to put the film plate beneath her. They quickly set up the placement for the X-ray, pulling the tube down over the woman's chest. They got it done in record time. The results were two nasty areas on her lungs, the right worse than the left.

Pneumonia. Just as Kaleb suspected.

"We need to start her on an azithromycin drip stat." Maddy glanced at Kaleb, who had stayed with the pair throughout everything that had happened. She couldn't blame him. Gloria had started off as his patient. "Can you get someone to make up a chart on her? Ask them to come up so that Mr. Lowell doesn't have to leave her side."

"I'm on it."

Soon they had Gloria in a room and hooked up to an IV that would pump strong antibiotics directly into her veins and hopefully fight off the infection raging in her lungs. If they didn't see improvement soon, they'd have to culture the bacteria and make some adjustments. Even as she jotted notes in her chart—with Gloria's husband seated in a chair next to her bed in ICU—the woman's eyes fluttered open. She immediately searched the room until her gaze fell on her husband's face. She gave a small nod as if reassuring herself that he really was there. Maddy wasn't about to break her promise to the woman.

She went over to the bed and explained what they'd done and what her treatment would be. Gloria seemed exhausted, but relieved. Maddy patted her hand. "You did the right thing by coming."

Gloria nodded again, her eyelids flickering shut.

"How long will she have to stay here?"

"Let's wait and see how those antibiotics do,

okay? We don't want her in here any longer than necessary. But we want to send her home healthy."

Clyde wrapped his fingers around his wife's. "Can I call my children from here or do I need to step outside?"

"You're fine. I made a promise to her. Let's not break it."

When Maddy had a moment to look around, she realized that Kaleb was no longer in the room. Her heart squeezed with disappointment. Had she really expected him to stick around indefinitely? He had his own job to do. Still. Something wished he'd at least warned her he was leaving.

Why? It shouldn't matter.

But it did.

With one last goodbye to the husband, she slipped the chart in the holder and pushed out of ICU.

"Hey, I thought you could use a coffee. You take it black, right?" The familiar voice startled her and she spun around to see Kaleb walking toward her, holding two paper cups emblazoned with the hospital cafeteria's emblem.

He remembered how she liked her coffee? She sighed and took the cup he offered her. "Yes. Thank you."

Taking a deep sip and letting the burn of the liquid anchor her back in the here and now, where life wasn't always as frantic as it had just been for the last hour or so, she said, "I thought you'd be long gone by now."

"I went to check on our accident victim from the kite festival."

That was right. Maddy had been following his progress as well. "Any news?"

"He's due to be released tomorrow, actually. The pin in his leg will be there for several more weeks, but he should make a complete recovery."

"That's wonderful news. I'm happy for him. I wish everyone had as good an outcome as he did."

"Me too." Kaleb rubbed the back of his neck. "Sometimes it doesn't work out that way."

"No."

"Do you have a few minutes?" he asked. "I know I acted weird the night we were together, and I'd like to explain why."

She glanced at her watch, shocked that it wasn't one hour that had passed but three since she'd first set foot in that hotel room. "I'm due to go off duty, actually, but I want to stick close for the next little while and make sure Gloria is doing okay. But we can go out to the garden, if you want."

There were benches there, and, although there was quite a bit of foot traffic, the seating was designed so that families could discuss matters of life and death without being easily overheard by those passing by. It was the perfect place, although she couldn't imagine what he wanted to say about that night.

Did she really want to hear his reasons? Yes. Maybe it would make her feel better about the whole thing. And she was somehow glad of the fact that he'd stayed around and bought her coffee.

He led her to the farthest reaches of the garden

and motioned for her to sit, which she did. "First of all, I owe you an apology."

There was a pause as she tried to process exactly what he was saying he was sorry about. Spending the night? Or leaving the way he had? "Could you be a little more specific?"

"My questions about Chloe. It was intrusive. Her…health…is none of my business."

It took her a minute to realize what he was talking about. "Her headache? I didn't think anything of it."

"Maybe you should." He leaned hard against the backrest of the bench. He chugged back some of his coffee, throat working in a way that made her wince. Her brew was still boiling hot.

Touching his arm, she waited until he put his cup back down. "What's going on, Kaleb? Are you worried I'll somehow try to pull the daddy card on you?"

"What? Oh, hell, no."

If anything, he looked even more uncomfortable, as if that was exactly what he'd been thinking. "If it makes you feel better, I'm not looking for a serious relationship. I don't want Chloe growing to love someone who isn't going to be a permanent part of my life. I thought we'd already settled that?"

"We had. I mean…I just wanted to explain why I made such a big deal over her headache."

Had he? Maddy certainly didn't remember it that way. "It's okay."

"It's not. But I want you to know why." He dragged a hand through his hair and then turned back toward her. "My daughter had headaches. Terrible ones."

Daughter? Maddy's mind churned to life at the unexpectedness of his words. She'd guessed that Kaleb had been married at one time, but he'd never once mentioned a child. But some of his behavior at her apartment made sense now. "Does she still have them?" Maybe he was going to suggest Chloe go to his own daughter's doctor.

"No, she doesn't still have them." His throat moved. "She died."

Shock held her immobile for a minute, and she actually had to shift her body a couple of times before she located her voice. "Oh, Kaleb, I'm so sorry. I had no idea."

"I never said anything, that's why." He rubbed a thumb over the rim of his cup. "She had cancer. Only we didn't know it. I kept…" He stopped. Took a deep breath. "I prescribed painkillers. Took her to a pediatrician while on vacation who assured me that a lot of kids her age get headaches. It was part of her circulatory system growing and changing. She'd grow out of them. Only she didn't. They just got worse."

Maddy's heart squeezed so tight she feared it would stop beating altogether. The reason for his reaction to Chloe's headache was horrifyingly clear now. She took a couple of careful breaths, trying to keep them steady. The last thing she needed was for her asthma to act up.

She tucked her hand inside the crook of his elbow and laid her head on his shoulder, needing to give him comfort and not sure how to. Was there really anything that could ease the pain of losing a child? "Was it very long ago?"

"Five years." His bicep tensed beneath her

hand. "My wife trusted me. I'm a doctor, for God's sake. It took a picture snapped at Christmas to raise the alarm. The dreaded red-eye effect. We laughed about it, planning to edit the image. But when I went to do just that a week later, I got to Grace's eyes and realized one of them glowed white instead of red. I got a horrible feeling in the pit of my stomach. And I knew. I knew." He paused as if gathering his thoughts, or maybe just to gather his courage to finish. "We went back to the doctor—a neurologist here at West Seattle this time. She diagnosed Grace with an aggressive form of retinoblastoma. It had already metastasized to her brain. Within three months she was gone, despite trying every treatment available."

The cure rate for retinoblastoma was pretty good, with the removal of the affected eye, but the aggressive types had a dismal prognosis. And those were normally inherited.

"And your wife?"

He gave a hard laugh. "She said she didn't blame me. Which was kind of ludicrous, since I blamed myself. Not only could I not diagnose my own child, I had a grandfather with a prosthetic eye. It should have tipped me off, but it didn't. I never put two and two together until after she died."

"It wasn't your fault, Kaleb. You had your daughter checked out. More than once."

"You don't understand. I gave it to her. Handed it to her on a silver genetic platter."

Maddy swallowed, trying to find the right words and failing. "You didn't. You didn't even know it was in your family. People aren't routinely screened unless there's a reason."

What it could mean, though, was that Kaleb might not be willing to risk having another child. She doubted she would. That made her chest hurt all the more.

"It could have been prevented, if I'd known."

"How? Would you have chosen not to have her?"

"No. Grace was…" His voice had an ominous wobble to it. "She was my life. Afterward,

Janice couldn't… She never looked at me the same way ever again."

Like Matthew, once he'd discovered she was pregnant?

No, this was nothing like that. But her lungs burned at the thought of Kaleb dealing with the collapse of his marriage even while he mourned his child.

Maddy set her cup on the bench beside her so she could wrap her other hand around his arm and hug it close. "I'm so, so sorry, Kaleb."

"I just wanted you to understand why I butted in the way I did."

"What can I do to help?" She wasn't sure what else to say. She allowed her fingers to stroke up his arm, trying to give whatever comfort she could.

He turned his head, meeting her eyes. "Somehow, I think you already did. I've never told anyone the whole story. Until now."

The brown had deepened slightly and his gaze dropped to her lips before coming back up. Her breath stuttered in her chest. He was thinking about kissing her?

Probably not.

Or maybe he was.

Suddenly, it didn't matter. Because she was going to take matters into her own hands. And right now, it had nothing to do with comforting him, or pitying him. It had everything to do with the way this man made her feel, whether he was happy, angry or mired in a pit of grief. She wanted him. Needed him. And if there was the slightest possibility that he felt the same way about her, she was going to grab it with both hands and hold on.

With those thoughts running through her head, Maddy slowly stretched up and touched her lips to his.

# CHAPTER TEN

THE DOOR SLAMMED open to her apartment and in an instant Kaleb had her trapped against the foyer wall, his mouth slanting over hers in a kiss that robbed her lungs of breath. Then he was shoving the top to her scrubs up and over her head, letting it fall to the ground. Her bra soon followed.

Maddy was just as desperate to get his clothes off. Before she'd had a chance to revel in the feel of his bare chest against hers, he backed up a step and stripped off his trousers, socks and shoes. He was soon naked in front of her. But he didn't rejoin her immediately.

"Wait right there."

"What? No." She went ahead and pushed her own scrubs down and kicked off her sensible, comfortable shoes. The last thing she wanted right now, though, was to be comfortable.

She wanted to be taken.

By this man.

He retrieved his wallet from his pants and found a foil-wrapped packet, his eyes slowly trailing down her body.

Liquid fire pumped through her veins. "Hurry."

He ripped the condom open with his teeth, but before he could remove it, Maddy moved forward, taking it from his hands and setting it on the padded bench to her left. "I changed my mind. We won't be needing that quite yet."

"Oh, no?" One brow went up. She was thankful there was no hint of fear in his voice. He trusted her to do the right thing. And she wouldn't chance putting him through what he'd suffered with his daughter. She wouldn't risk a pregnancy.

The fact that he knew she wouldn't, though, sent an ache shimmering through her gut. Pushing past it, she slid her fingers over his shoulders and pressed her body tight against his, loving the sensation of her curves settling into the hard planes of his torso and hips. And that pulsing flesh against her belly found a matching need inside her.

The human body was exquisitely designed.

"I thought you wanted to hurry."

She laughed. "You're like an expensive box of chocolates. Much too good to swallow all at once." The naughty words hung in the air, eliciting a response from a certain part of his anatomy that made her grin. It was as if they'd never had that difficult conversation in the hospital garden. And that was just what she wanted. To help him forget, if only for a few moments.

"Maddy…" The warning in his voice sounded very real. And she loved it.

When she planted a kiss on his left shoulder, he didn't try to stop her. Nor when she trailed down past his pec. Or his abdomen, although the muscles in it jumped at her touch. The real test came when she bent her knees and slowly glided down until she knelt in front of him.

"Don't do this." This time his words sounded half strangled.

"Are you telling me no, Doctor?" And if he

was? Maybe he was one of those rare guys who saw oral sex as something to be reviled. If he did, she would be disappointed, but she would still make love to him. On his terms. She was willing to compromise, if necessary. But, oh, how she wanted to…

"No." His Adam's apple took a quick dip. "I'm not telling you no."

She smiled, allowing her tongue to dance across her mouth in preparation. "Well, in that case…"

Her lips parted around him, the warm, taut flesh brushing across her tongue. Her ex had demanded she do this. But Kaleb seemed to almost fear it. Which was why she wanted to so badly. To erase the memories of shame and ridicule and replace them with good ones. Healthy ones. With a man who had no expectations. No hidden agendas. No trying to force her in subtle and not-so-subtle ways.

She let herself enjoy it. Each hiss of air that sounded above her drove her almost wild with need. She wanted to push him over the edge, wanted to take him deeper. To—

Hands on her shoulders gave a light squeeze and edged her backward, her lips leaving him with an audible pop. She licked them again.

"If you're trying to kill me, Maddy, you're doing a hell of a job."

She wasn't trying to kill him. Just hoped to make him want her as much as she wanted him. And from the look in his eyes, she might very well have succeeded.

"Come here."

When she tried to slide forward again as if misunderstanding him, the grip on her shoulders tightened slightly. "Up here. All the way up here."

He held out his hands to help her, her body tingling with need. Foreplay didn't need long sessions of heavy petting, evidently, because she felt as if she were going to explode the second he touched her. And touch her he did. Soon she was off her feet and on her bed.

Kaleb pushed inside her with a quick thrust that had her writhing beneath him, the sensation of fullness almost overwhelming.

"Again." She arched up to meet him this time,

needing to reach the peak quickly…needing him to take her there.

Gripping his shoulders, she didn't let him slow the pace, and when he tried to, she shoved him until he was flat on his back. Then she rode him hard, exulting in the echoed need on his face—at the hands that reached to pull her close, to kiss her, even as she was tumbling over the edge, her world on fire. Two more thrusts and he joined her, breathing out her name as she took everything he had and tried to give it back to him.

And just like that, Maddy realized she was done. Over. Kaput.

She loved him. And this time there was no going back.

It couldn't be this easy. Could it? Over a week had gone by and their trip to the Space Needle was here. Chloe stood beside him on the observation deck, practically buzzing with excitement as she looked out over the huge city.

Surprisingly, Maddy had let him spend the last couple of days in their company, despite her earlier statements about not wanting the little girl to get attached.

Maybe Maddy had been worried about the wrong person all along. Because he was attached. To Maddy. To Chloe. Even Roxy had an odd-ball charm to her that made him shrug off things that would have ordinarily irritated him. Like her question this morning about whether or not he was as into Maddy as she was evidently into him.

Maddy had gone red to her very roots, while shooting her sister looks that threatened death and dismemberment if she didn't shut up. Not that it stopped Roxy for even a second.

Some things had clicked inside Kaleb after he'd made love to Maddy. First, he'd made love to her at her place again. And he hadn't died. Or even fainted. And he'd been more than happy to spend the night, except that Maddy had shooed him on his way, saying she had to pick Chloe up from Roxy's. When he'd called her the next night to ask if they could rent a movie and watch it to-gether—the three of them—Maddy hadn't told him to get lost. She'd simply read the name of a movie she and Chloe had been hoping to see. He'd shown up at her door with said movie and takeout.

Chloe had curled up next to him and fallen asleep halfway through the movie. And the look Maddy had given him… Well, it had taken his breath away. He'd picked the little girl up and carried her back to her tiny bedroom and tucked her in, Jetta settling in on top of the covers. Maddy had watched him from the doorway, a funny expression in her eyes. That night, she'd let him sleep in her bed, only asking that he be out before Chloe woke up.

He was.

The same thing had happened the next evening. And the next. Kaleb found himself anticipating what Maddy would say, or found himself recognizing the way her eyes crinkled when he said something he knew she'd laugh at.

This was his first outing with Chloe, Roxy and Maddy since the kite festival. He'd been nervous.

Roxy was not.

And Maddy was… Well, the woman was hot.

And sweet. And nothing at all like Janice. In a good way. Because whereas Janice had worn sweetness like a costume, it had collapsed in the face of crisis, much like that slinky cat suit that Maddy had donned, which was discarded at the end of the day. Maddy's sweetness went to the core of who she was—had survived an abusive husband.

She touched his hand, pulling him from his thoughts. "Everything okay?"

"Yes. Very okay." He threaded his fingers through hers. The catch he heard in her breath was very real, but she didn't try to pull away. Even when Chloe grabbed his other hand and held on tight. Roxy had walked on ahead, throwing him a knowing smile. It also held a hint of warning: *hurt either of them, and you'll pay.*

The last thing he wanted to do was hurt Maddy. Or Chloe.

"We're way high, aren't we, Kaleb?" Chloe strained at the railing.

"We are way high." His eyes, though, were on Maddy. Their relationship had been climbing as surely as the elevator that had climbed the steel girders of the building and dumped them out at he pinnacle. A fall from this height would be devastating.

Kaleb had no intention of falling, though. If ne had to come back down, he intended to do t slowly and steadily, the same way he'd come.

Roxy stood several feet away from them taking pictures. The only glitch to an otherwise perfect day was that Maddy seemed to be going out of her way to stay out of the shots that her sister ined up that included him. Still protecting herself from being hurt?

He couldn't blame her. But something about it oothered him. Normally it was Kaleb who sidestepped any hint of being linked with a particular female. He wasn't used to the reverse happening. He didn't like it. Especially when Maddy was the one doing it. Maybe she was afraid.

The way he'd once been?

Did that mean he no longer was?

He had no idea. And today wasn't the day to go down that particular avenue. It could wait for another place. Another time. When he was alone with her and they could talk freely.

Maybe he should ask Roxy if she could watch Chloe for a couple of hours tomorrow.

So he could do what?

He wasn't sure. Make a decision? Possibly. All he knew was that he wasn't ready for whatever they had to end. He hoped Maddy felt the same way. It seemed that there'd been a change over the last week. Even his nightmares had faded, disappearing completely whenever he shared Maddy's bed.

Surely she had experienced the same freedom? Otherwise she wouldn't have let him stay the last couple of nights.

Except she was avoiding being in a picture with him today. Maybe he should straight-out ask her.

Squeezing her hand, he leaned closer. "Embarrassed to be seen with me?"

"What?" Her green-eyed gaze swung around to meet him.

"I noticed that you don't want Roxy to catch us together."

"Oh…" Her face turned pink. "It's just that my mom…"

"Your mom…?"

"I don't want her thinking there are things there that aren't."

He paused. Maybe the altitude was affecting his brain, but he suddenly wanted to lay it out there. "What if they are?"

Chloe swung her arm back and forth, still holding his hand. "What's there?"

"Nothing." Kaleb said it at the exact same time as Maddy. They both laughed. Only the laughter felt a little more hollow than it had earlier.

"Hey, guys," Roxy called. "I don't know about you, but I'm starving. Anyone ready to eat?"

"Me!" Chloe let go of him and ran over to hug her aunt.

Maddy glanced at him. "I guess it's time for lunch." She hooked pinkies with him and squeezed for a second before releasing his hand. It felt right. Comforting. Like an acknowledgment that needed no words after all. He tweaked a lock of her hair in return. And this time when

Roxy spun around to take a picture with her phone, Maddy didn't try to duck out of it.

The perfect ending to a perfect outing.

"Mommy, my head hurts again."

They'd just finished lunch and were waiting on Kaleb to bring the car around to get them. The day had been beyond fun. Kaleb had been attentive and charming, entertaining them with stories from his childhood and medical school. For the first time since she was a teenager, Maddy felt as if things were working out in her favor. That included her move to Seattle, which had definitely been the right decision.

"Is it worse?" Chloe had commented that morning that she didn't feel well, that her head was kind of achy. Maddy had given her some acetaminophen this morning as a precaution, and she'd seemed well enough during the day. Maybe the change in pressure from the trip up the Space Needle and then back down had bothered her sinuses or something.

"Yes."

She did look a little pale, and when Maddy put her hand on her daughter's forehead, she felt warm. Maybe it was her imagination. It was muggy out today, despite the breeze.

She glanced at her sister. "Can you feel her head for me?"

Roxy knelt in front of Chloe. "What's wrong, munchkin? Feeling a little under the weather?"

"It's my stupid head."

Her sister grinned. "You shouldn't call yourself a stupid head."

Chloe tried to smile, but it was obvious something was wrong. Even Roxy seemed worried. "I think she might have a fever."

That would explain the headache. And Chloe's preschool teacher had said there was a stomach bug or something going around and not to be surprised if she caught it.

"Where does it hurt, honey?"

"My whole head."

Moving behind her daughter, she put her fingertips on Chloe's temples and rubbed in slow circles the way she did when the little girl had a migraine. If they could just get her home, she could get some more medicine in her and maybe ward off a full-blown attack.

Kaleb pulled up to the curb, climbing from the car in order to open doors for them. He glanced at Maddy and then down at Chloe. "Everything okay?"

"I think she's getting a migraine."

Her daughter chose that very second to vomit everything she'd eaten all over the sidewalk.

Damn. She hadn't thought to bring anything with them, and Chloe had seemed fine until a few minutes ago.

Kaleb fished some napkins out of his glove compartment and handed them to her. He seemed a little pale himself. But Maddy didn't have time to worry about him. She cleaned Chloe up the best she could, feeling terrible about leaving behind a mess, but there was nothing she could do about it at the moment.

"I just need to get her home."

They climbed into the car, and this time Maddy sat in back with her daughter, moving to the middle so she could soothe the girl, while Roxy got into the front. Within twenty minutes they were at her apartment building. By that time, Maddy was seriously worried. Chloe seemed listless and her fever had shot up.

Before Kaleb could pull into the complex, she leaned forward to touch his shoulder. "I hate to ask you this, but would you mind driving us to the hospital?"

Roxy twisted around in her seat, took one look at Chloe and let out a soft cry. "I've never seen her this bad before."

"No. Me either." In fact, Maddy's heart was pounding in her chest and she was feeling a queasiness of her own.

In the rearview mirror, Kaleb's eyes met hers. Then he said, "Hold on tight."

He'd wanted to stay with them during the examination, but couldn't bring himself to. The Chloe who had arrived at the hospital had been nothing like the Chloe who had been clutching his hand on the observation deck. Dread pumped through his system along with a feeling of déjà vu.

*This isn't Grace. Maddy told you herself that Chloe suffers from periodic migraines.*

The look of fear on Roxy's face had said it all, though. This was no ordinary migraine.

He sat behind his desk and opened a drawer. Grace's picture was buried in the bottommost recesses beneath paperwork and medical periodicals. He dug deep, his fingers probing as if knowing exactly where he'd find her.

There.

Closing around the simple metal frame, they pulled out the picture of his two-year-old daughter. Brown pigtails and a bright blue-eyed smile met his gaze. She looked like Janice in so many ways. An ache settled deep in his chest. What if what was wrong with Chloe was more than a simple migraine?

Could he go through what had happened with Grace a second time? It was one of the reasons he'd sequestered himself in the office by himself.

Trying to drum up the nerve to go out there and support Maddy, who must be frantic by now.

What if he made things worse? What if his past came out at the worst possible moment and made Maddy needlessly fear for her daughter's life? What if his reactions and facial expressions did that every single time she showed the faintest twinge or pain or suffered from the flu?

What if his fear of losing Chloe turned Maddy into a neurotic mess? He'd already seen how his questions had sowed seeds of doubt in her mind. Would it do the same to Chloe? Force her to live in fear, instead of enjoying her childhood?

Could he do that to her? To Maddy?

Could he do that to himself?

Those questions held him captive in his chair. Even when Roxy had knocked on the door and peeked her head in, asking him to come out and see Chloe, he'd sat there, so afraid of making things worse for everyone. She must have seen the answer in his face, because when she'd opened her mouth to say something else, she'd snapped it shut again.

She'd left without a word and hadn't returned. What the hell was happening down there?

He hadn't heard from anyone in over an hour.

*Pick up the phone and call her, you jerk.*

He toyed with the corner of Grace's photo frame, hoping against hope he would wake up and find out that the last several hours had just been a dream, the return of those nightmares where Grace's face had been replaced by Chloe's. Only this was very real. And Grace was still gone.

And Chloe?

Hell. He picked up the phone and called the nurses' station in the pediatric wing. Someone answered, but he didn't recognize the woman's name. When she asked if she could help him, he somehow grunted out his name and that he was calling about Chloe Grimes.

The silence on the other end of the line was deafening.

He stood to his feet, fingers fisting around the phone. "Hello?"

Her voice finally came back. "I'm sorry. I was

just checking something. I have a note here to let you know that Dr. Kline is still with her. Chloe has a migraine compounded by a stomach virus. She's getting some IV fluids, but she should be fine in a few days."

The wave of relief that went over him made him collapse back into his chair, even as the nurse's voice continued. "Would you like me to get Dr. Grimes? I'm sure she wouldn't mind stepping out—"

"No, thank you. I'll speak with her another time." The churning in his gut told him he was in no shape to talk to Maddy or anyone right now.

He pushed the end button on his cell phone. Then, looking at Grace's picture one last time, he lifted the paperwork in the bottom drawer and gently laid it back in its resting place. He had his answer, and he knew what he was going to do. Chloe was perfectly fine. This had just been an ordinary migraine. But he knew that his reaction today would be the same every single time something happened. He would blow things way out of proportion and fear the worst. And doing that would help no one. Not him. Not Maddy. And certainly not Chloe, who deserved to grow up in a secure household, free from a neurotic mess of a man. A man who couldn't seem to shake his demons no matter how hard he tried.

Finally talking his legs into getting up from his chair, he slowly walked out of his office and headed for the nearest exit.

# CHAPTER ELEVEN

HER MOM'S COAXING had finally worked. Maddy was back in Gamble Point. She and Chloe.

Maddy needed time to heal. To think about where she'd been and where she wanted to go. So far, though, nothing had clicked into place.

Chloe tugged at her hand as they stood in the kitchen. "When are we going home? I miss Aunt Roxy, and Kaleb hasn't called me. Not even once."

Maddy gritted her teeth, but somehow managed to force out a cheerful answer. "I know, honey. But I'm sure Dr. McBride is busy."

So far he'd been "busy" every time Chloe had asked about him over the last two weeks. It had been a lie, but one she'd been forced to repeat time and time again. In reality, she had no idea if he was busy or not. In fact, she had no idea where Kaleb even was, and she didn't care.

Her mom was thrilled to have them back. Only the house she'd grown up in didn't feel very much like home anymore. She hadn't made a definitive move yet, as far as making any kind of decisions, and she wasn't quite sure what she was waiting on.

A miracle?

Well, that ship had already sailed.

Kaleb had rejected Chloe in her hour of need and, in doing so, he'd rejected her too. She'd warned herself time and time again that she was allowing Kaleb to get too close, and was letting her daughter get too attached. And yet she'd allowed things to continue, going as far as to let the man stay in her house—while her daughter was in the other room.

How could she have been so very stupid?

He'd called the nurses' station to check on Chloe, yes. At least according to the woman who'd been manning the main desk. But when asked if he wanted to speak to her, Kaleb had said no.

No!

Although the attending pediatrician had suspected meningitis at first, Chloe's headache had been nothing more than one of her migraines combined with a stomach virus. But what if it had been something more serious? Kaleb hadn't been able to bring himself to travel two floors to the pediatric wing to check on her.

She was sorry his daughter had died. Sorry that he blamed himself for what had happened. Lord only knew that she was still dealing with the aftereffects of Matthew's suicide. But she was finally ready to move forward, and she'd hoped that Kaleb was too.

But if she'd needed to know how he would respond in an emergency, she had her answer. He would withdraw into a shell and then walk away without a word. The same way he'd walked out of the hospital that day.

Her mom came into the farmhouse, a basket full of tomatoes in her arms. Maddy took them from her and set them on the counter. "You shouldn't be doing that by yourself."

"And you should unpack your bags. You've been here for two weeks, honey. If I didn't know better, I'd think you were waiting for someone to come and take you back to Seattle."

"Of course I'm not. I just haven't gotten around to it. That's all."

She wasn't waiting. Because even if Kaleb showed up in the flesh, she doubted he could convince her to go back with him, unless he got down on bended knee.

And maybe not even then. So why was she picturing him doing just that?

Her mom came over and pressed her cheek against hers. Maddy breathed in the familiar scents that she'd grown up with: rich soil, fresh vegetables and her mom's lilac perfume. Good clean smells that should be welcoming and comforting. And they were. But more as a landing pad to get her bearings before being shot back out into the world. Only this time she had no idea where she would wind up. Maybe she should just stay here in Gamble Point. Her mother would love it.

As if reading her mind, her mom gave her a quick hug. "Why don't I give you some time alone to work through some things?" She held out her hand to Chloe. "Do you want to go help your grandma feed some chickens?"

"Yes!" Chloe started to run toward the door only to stop and look back at her mother, as if uncertain if Maddy would be okay by herself.

Her eyes flooded with tears. Her daughter should not have to worry about anything more than chickens.

She forced herself to smile. "Go ahead. Maybe we can go get some ice cream when you come back."

With that, her mother and her daughter went out the door hand in hand.

A deep ache settled into her chest. Where was she going to go from here?

Back to Seattle? And see Kaleb there and wonder why he hadn't been able to see past his own hurt to someone else's?

Ha! As she'd done? She hadn't been able to see past what Matthew had done all those years ago. Instead, she'd assumed that Kaleb—and every other man—would do the exact same things: abandon her and Chloe in their hour of need.

Hadn't Kaleb done exactly that?

Yes. He had.

Roxy had told her not to leave. To give him a chance to realize he'd been wrong. "He's a groveler, you know. Deep down, he is. You just need to give him some time to get those old knee hinges oiled and back in working order."

Instead, Maddy had packed her bags and had left Seattle, turning her caseload over to other doctors. She'd wanted to hand in her resignation, but the hospital administrator had asked her to take a few weeks of personal vacation time instead.

So that was what she'd done. She'd left Jetta in the care of Roxy. Just in case.

And her bags were still packed in her childhood bedroom. Why? Did she really expect Kaleb to swoop in on a white horse and rescue her?

No, because she didn't need rescuing. She was a strong woman who'd done just fine on her own. But what she'd wanted was for him to come through for her. Had felt as if she needed him to.

Except she was afraid that Roxy might have been right for once in her life. Maybe she hadn't given Kaleb enough time to deal with everything that had happened between them.

Should she go and storm back into his life, demanding that he hear her out? And if, afterward, he said he didn't want to make room in his heart for her and Chloe?

Well, then he could damn well tell her that to her face.

Oh, yes. He definitely could.

*That* was why her bags were still packed. Because she wasn't quite ready to give up on the place—or the person—she'd left behind. Not until she knew for sure that it…that *he*…didn't want her to stay.

She could start by calling an end to the private party she'd been having in Pity City and making a plane reservation for the earliest possible date.

She was still on the phone with the travel agency when the doorbell rang. She glanced at the back door, hoping she'd see her mother outside, but there was nothing but acres of crops there. The henhouse was about a hundred yards to the south.

Damn.

"I'm sorry. I'll need to call you back in a few minutes."

It was probably either a delivery or one of her mom's field workers with a question. Sliding her phone into the back pocket of her jeans, she headed for the door. She swung it open, ready to tell whoever it was that her mom was out feeding her chickens, except it wasn't a worker.

And it wasn't a deliveryman, but he was carrying a small bag.

Kaleb.

She blinked. Opened her eyes.

Nope. Still there.

"May I come in?"

She swallowed. How could he be here when she'd just been thinking of him?

"Of course." She stepped back so that he could come inside. "What are you doing here?"

He set the bag on the floor. "I'll get to that. First, is Chloe okay?"

For a split second, she thought something had happened out in the chicken coop, then realized he was just asking in generalities. Her voice cooled. "Yes. She's fine. But of course you know that."

"Roxy filled me in on what happened. I'm sorry I left the way I did." He toed the bag, but his eyes didn't leave hers.

If he thought she was going to make this easy for him, he was wrong. Yes, she'd been ready to go back to Seattle and demand an explanation, but some of her resolve was wavering now that they were face-to-face. Still, she had to see this through, so she took a deep breath and let him have it.

"You hurt me, Kaleb. You hurt Chloe. We needed you, and you walked away."

He nodded. "I know. And I have no excuse, other than to say it's the first time since Grace's death that I've had to face the possibility of losing someone else I'd come to care about."

"So you thought it was better to turn your back on us instead?"

"Yes. It was stupid and cowardly, but I was also afraid that my past might poison anything we could have together. As a family."

"A family?" Her heart skipped a beat. "I don't understand."

"Every time Chloe feels an ache or has a simple headache, I can't guarantee I won't leap to the worst possible conclusion. The thought of forcing you both to live in fear—to witness what I become during those times…" He stopped, a muscle working in his jaw. "I thought it might be in everyone's best interest if I just left you in peace. But the reality is, I couldn't bring myself to stay away. And when I went to find you a few days later, they told me you'd left."

"You didn't try to call."

"No. I told myself I had my answer. I should just let you go. It was better for everyone." He took a step forward. "But I'm not so sure that's the truth. Because it's not better for me. And I'm hoping it's not better for you."

She swallowed, trying to get rid of the lump in her throat. "I haven't decided yet."

"Would it change things if I told you I love you? That I love Chloe?"

She wanted nothing more than to fling herself into his arms, but she couldn't live with someone who burned hot one minute and cold the next. She'd been there, and it pretty much sucked. "And the next time Chloe has a migraine? Or a stomachache? Will you leave again?"

He reached out and took her hand. "I'm not going to lie, Maddy. It'll scare the hell out of me. And I'll want to run. Every single time. You'll have to help me not to."

"How will I do that?"

A tiny thread of hope began unwinding in her heart, just like the string on their kite at the festival. He loved her. He'd admitted it. Wasn't that enough?

He reached into the bag at his feet and pulled

out two small jewelers' boxes. They were identical in every way. He held one out to her. "Open it."

Heart pounding, she took the box from him. Clicking up the lid, she found a heart-shaped ring nestled in a bed of gray velvet. "I don't understand."

He took the box from her and unearthed the ring. "It's a promise ring. A promise that I'll stay, no matter how scared I am. No matter how tough the road ahead might seem. A promise that I'll be there for you. And for Chloe. The second box has a ring just like this one. For her. Roxy gave me your sizes."

"But how...?"

"She called your mom, who measured your fingers while you slept."

Maddy glanced at the door. "She knew you were coming. That's why..."

All that talk about unpacking suitcases had been just that. Talk. Her mom and her sister had known what she wanted before she did.

She loved this man.

But could she trust him? Could she believe he

would be there for her and Chloe, no matter how hard it got? She took the ring from his hand and toyed with it. She caught a glint of something inside the band. She turned the ring to the light to make it out.

*My heart. My love. My life. No matter what.*

Her eyes prickled, moisture coming to them and then spilling over.

Kaleb touched the second box. "Chloe's ring says the same thing. But I wanted to talk to you alone before she saw it."

"Roxy was in on this?"

He nodded. "I tracked her down when I couldn't find you. For a week, she refused to return my calls, and when she finally did, I had to convince her that everything I just told you was the truth." He smiled. "She put me through the wringer."

Maddy could well imagine. Was that why Roxy had told her he was a groveler? "What did she make you do?"

"You'll see in just a minute." His fingers reached out for hers again, twining their hands together. "I asked Roxy to call your mom and have her take Chloe outside, in case you told me to get the hell out of here."

He lifted her hand and kissed it. "I'm hoping you'll ask me to stay instead."

Maddy scrubbed her palm over her face before closing her fingers around the ring. "I'm not going to ask you to do that. I want you to go."

When he flinched, she hurried to cup his face in her hands. "You misunderstood. I want you to go, because I want to go with you." She closed her eyes, love and relief pouring through her. "I want to go home to Seattle."

He didn't move for a long second, and then he was crushing her to him, kissing her, murmuring words she didn't understand with her ears, but felt with her heart.

When he finally let her come up for air, he took her right hand and slid the ring over her finger. "So is this a yes?"

"It is. Roxy promised me you were a good groveler, but that you were just a little rusty. She was right."

He smiled. "Ah, so that's what she meant. She told me when the time was right I would understand." He reached back into the bag and pulled out an old-fashioned oil can. "She told me I should take this can and apply the contents liberally."

"I bet she did."

Kaleb tunneled his fingers through her hair. "She was right. I'm a great groveler, and I plan to grovel for the rest of my life, if you'll let me. I love you, Maddy."

"I love you too. But maybe we'll keep the oil can around, just in case." Wrapping her arms around his neck, she hugged him close. "Take us home."

"I need to tell you something that might make you change your mind." The words were hesitant enough that they made her lean back to look at his face. "I had genetic counseling after Grace's death and it confirmed I carry the gene for retinoblastoma. I promised myself I wouldn't have any more children. If that makes you decide you don't want me, I'll understand."

Did he really think that made any difference at all? Maybe she wasn't the only one who needed reassurance.

"There are other ways to have children. Or not. Whatever we decide about that, it won't change the way I feel. Ever. I want you. I always will."

He pressed his cheek against hers, the way her mom had done just moments earlier. Only this time she felt moisture on her skin. Tears. And just beneath the salty tang, she caught the faint medicinal scent carried by hospitals everywhere, and Kaleb's musky aftershave.

But most of all, he smelled like Home.

# EPILOGUE

THE KITE HUNG suspended from the ceiling in Chloe's room.

Gone was the tiny twin bed in the revamped study of Maddy's old place. A year's worth of hard work and counseling on Kaleb's part had brought him to the place where his heart no longer clamped tight in fear whenever Chloe got one of her headaches or Maddy's asthma came out to play.

Even before he finished therapy, though, Maddy had allowed him to put a simple gold band on her left hand, a sign of faith that she believed he was there to stay. And he was. He'd moved them into his apartment. Jetta was probably the hardest sell, but even the cat had decided the new digs weren't all that bad. Especially with the catwalk Kaleb had installed on the veranda, which gave him a wonderful view of the city below.

Chloe was at school until four o'clock. They'd taken full advantage of that time together, since time was in short supply these days. He tightened the towel around his waist and surveyed Maddy's handiwork. She'd made his house a home. And not just for him.

Right on cue, a sharp cry shattered the peaceful atmosphere. Making his way down the hallway, he intercepted Maddy, a bottle already in her hand.

"We timed that just right, didn't we?" Her grin was aimed at the towel.

"I don't know if it was our timing, or if she was just having mercy on us."

Together they went into the bedroom of another little girl. Rosa Jane. She wasn't theirs, but she'd already won over their hearts.

Kaleb wouldn't have any more biological children, but that didn't mean that he and Maddy couldn't provide love…and a secure home for children in need. They'd become foster parents, and Rosa Jane was their very first charge. If things went the way they hoped, she might even become a permanent member of their family.

Maddy picked the baby up from her crib and cuddled her in her arms. Trusting blue eyes blinked up at them as Kaleb put his arm around his wife's waist.

This was where he belonged. Here with Maddy, Chloe and whomever else fate might add to their home.

He kissed the top of her head, his heart brimming with a happiness he'd never dreamed possible. But she made it possible.

"Let me take her," he murmured.

"Are you sure?"

"Yes." He gathered the baby and her bottle and settled into the rocking chair in the corner. Maddy leaned against the door and watched as Rosa Jane greedily sucked at the milk.

"I think we can throw away that oil can."

It took him a minute to realize what she was talking about. He'd placed Roxy's oil can on a shelf in his office as a reminder to never let himself get rusty when it came to their relationship. "You never know. I might need it someday."

"I don't think so." She smiled and drew in a deep breath, letting it out in an audible sigh. "I think, Kaleb…I think we're going to be just fine without it. All of us."

\* \* \* \* \*

*If you enjoyed this story, check out these other great reads from Tina Beckett*
*WINNING BACK HIS DOCTOR BRIDE*
*PLAYBOY DOC'S MISTLETOE KISS*
*HOT DOC FROM HER PAST*
*HER PLAYBOY'S SECRET*

*All available now!*

# MILLS & BOON®
## Large Print Medical

## April

| | |
|---|---|
| Waking Up to Dr Gorgeous | Emily Forbes |
| Swept Away by the Seductive Stranger | Amy Andrews |
| One Kiss in Tokyo... | Scarlet Wilson |
| The Courage to Love Her Army Doc | Karin Baine |
| Reawakened by the Surgeon's Touch | Jennifer Taylor |
| Second Chance with Lord Branscombe | Joanna Neil |

## May

| | |
|---|---|
| The Nurse's Christmas Gift | Tina Beckett |
| The Midwife's Pregnancy Miracle | Kate Hardy |
| Their First Family Christmas | Alison Roberts |
| The Nightshift Before Christmas | Annie O'Neil |
| Started at Christmas... | Janice Lynn |
| Unwrapped by the Duke | Amy Ruttan |

## June

| | |
|---|---|
| White Christmas for the Single Mum | Susanne Hampton |
| A Royal Baby for Christmas | Scarlet Wilson |
| Playboy on Her Christmas List | Carol Marinelli |
| The Army Doc's Baby Bombshell | Sue MacKay |
| The Doctor's Sleigh Bell Proposal | Susan Carlisle |
| Christmas with the Single Dad | Louisa Heaton |

# MILLS & BOON®
## Large Print Medical

## July

| | |
|---|---|
| Falling for Her Wounded Hero | Marion Lennox |
| The Surgeon's Baby Surprise | Charlotte Hawkes |
| Santiago's Convenient Fiancée | Annie O'Neil |
| Alejandro's Sexy Secret | Amy Ruttan |
| The Doctor's Diamond Proposal | Annie Claydon |
| Weekend with the Best Man | Leah Martyn |

## August

| | |
|---|---|
| Their Meant-to-Be Baby | Caroline Anderson |
| A Mummy for His Baby | Molly Evans |
| Rafael's One Night Bombshell | Tina Beckett |
| Dante's Shock Proposal | Amalie Berlin |
| A Forever Family for the Army Doc | Meredith Webber |
| The Nurse and the Single Dad | Dianne Drake |

## September

| | |
|---|---|
| Their Secret Royal Baby | Carol Marinelli |
| Her Hot Highland Doc | Annie O'Neil |
| His Pregnant Royal Bride | Amy Ruttan |
| Baby Surprise for the Doctor Prince | Robin Gianna |
| Resisting Her Army Doc Rival | Sue MacKay |
| A Month to Marry the Midwife | Fiona McArthur |

# MILLS & BOON®
## Large Print – April 2017

## ROMANCE

| | |
|---|---|
| **A Di Sione for the Greek's Pleasure** | Kate Hewitt |
| **The Prince's Pregnant Mistress** | Maisey Yates |
| **The Greek's Christmas Bride** | Lynne Graham |
| **The Guardian's Virgin Ward** | Caitlin Crews |
| **A Royal Vow of Convenience** | Sharon Kendrick |
| **The Desert King's Secret Heir** | Annie West |
| **Married for the Sheikh's Duty** | Tara Pammi |
| **Winter Wedding for the Prince** | Barbara Wallace |
| **Christmas in the Boss's Castle** | Scarlet Wilson |
| **Her Festive Doorstep Baby** | Kate Hardy |
| **Holiday with the Mystery Italian** | Ellie Darkins |

## HISTORICAL

| | |
|---|---|
| **Bound by a Scandalous Secret** | Diane Gaston |
| **The Governess's Secret Baby** | Janice Preston |
| **Married for His Convenience** | Eleanor Webster |
| **The Saxon Outlaw's Revenge** | Elisabeth Hobbes |
| **In Debt to the Enemy Lord** | Nicole Locke |

## MEDICAL

| | |
|---|---|
| **Waking Up to Dr Gorgeous** | Emily Forbes |
| **Swept Away by the Seductive Stranger** | Amy Andrews |
| **One Kiss in Tokyo...** | Scarlet Wilson |
| **The Courage to Love Her Army Doc** | Karin Baine |
| **Reawakened by the Surgeon's Touch** | Jennifer Taylor |
| **Second Chance with Lord Branscombe** | Joanna Neil |

0317 GEN STD LP

# MILLS & BOON®

## Why shop at millsandboon.co.uk?

Each year, thousands of romance readers find their perfect read at millsandboon.co.uk. That's because we're passionate about bringing you the very best romantic fiction. Here are some of the advantages of shopping at www.millsandboon.co.uk:

∗ **Get new books first**—you'll be able to buy your favourite books one month before they hit the shops

∗ **Get exclusive discounts**—you'll also be able to buy our specially created monthly collections, with up to 50% off the RRP

∗ **Find your favourite authors**—latest news, interviews  and new releases for all your favourite authors and series on our website, plus ideas for what to try next

∗ **Join in**—once you've bought your favourite books, don't forget to register with us to rate, review and join in the discussions

Visit **www.millsandboon.co.uk**
for all this and more today!

Leabharlanna Poiblí Chathair Bhaile Átha Cliath
Dublin City Public Libraries